Rolling

By the same author

It Might Have Been Jerusalem

Rolling

Thomas Healy

Polygon
EDINBURGH

© Thomas Healy 1992

First published by Polygon
22 George Square
Edinburgh

Set in Monotype Sabon
by DSC Ltd, Cornwall
and printed and bound in Great Britain
by Redwood Press, Melksham, Wilts

British Library Cataloguing in Publication Data

Healy, Thomas, 1944–
Rolling.
I. Title
823.914 [F]

ISBN 0 7486 6121 2

The Publisher acknowledges subsidy from the Scottish Arts Council
towards the publication of this volume.

For my mother, Margaret,
and in memory of my father, John Healy.

All characters and events in this book are purely fictitious.

I remember Spain, a day in Barcelona, the statue of Columbus, and I was twenty-five years old then, that day—one to remember, for a hangover not to believe. Sweat popped my head to fill my eyes and I felt as if I were walking under water. I walked, head to the ground, three days in a whorehouse; a place with a fiddler, full barrels of wine and each step I took I thought to fall.

There would be other days, worse days, but that day, a stumbling lurch; I shook so that I could not smoke or hold a light, as, in a bar, I could barely lift the glass. Brandy. How I got the first one down I do not know. Standing. At the bar. A long brown counter. But spilling half of it I ordered another, glass filled to the brim and a bit steadier spilled only a little. The third brandy I was able to carry to a seat at the back of the place and, like a hobo, the start of a beard, sat puzzling. Just what had happened to me?

I had come on a day-trip to Barcelona. With a girl. From our hotel in Tossa. But where was she? I could remember boarding the bus, the journey in, the waterfront statue of Columbus, a bar or two, but nothing more. My mind was a blank. Total. Until the whorehouse—flashes of the whorehouse, and how the fuck had I landed there?

Sitting in that bar swigging the brandy, a bottle of beer, and I knew the name of the hotel in Tossa and thought to

phone but was scared to phone. Indeed I had visions of
Jean—my girl—dead, strangled in an alley and strangled by
me. Dear Jesus. If I had had black-outs before, missing
hours, they were nothing like this, three days or four.

After a few more drinks I raised the nerve and telephoned
Tossa.

Jean, a mighty release, for truly I thought—though I don't
know why—to have murdered her, came on the line.

'It's me,' I said.

'I know,' she said.

'I got drunk.'

'Where are you?'

'Barcelona. I'm still in Barcelona.'

'You're okay?'

'I think so.'

I got back to Tossa and was violently ill: the sweats,
shakes. But recovered by shifts to discover a dose of a
virulent clap that I inflicted on Jean—it required a drink to
recover from that.

We ended the holiday in separate rooms, and coming
home, on the plane, we sat apart.

I did not speak to Jean again, though I saw her sometimes—and sometimes, drunk, remembering, I would laugh.
On the day she was married I laughed. Drank whisky and
beer and howled a gale. But inside, the reel of my head,
scattered wits, a creeping sadness that I could not finger or
figure out. I did not, had never loved Jean. But screwed-up
somehow, a mighty ache, a jolly man, I drank to oblivion.

I was born in the Gorbals, Glasgow in 1944. I began I think
a timorous child, which was no good in that place, the old
tenements, where you had to fight; seven, eight years old
you had to fight, that or endure the tag of a sissy. So I fought,
though then, I hated to fight. It was better than the tag of a
sissy. But just kid's stuff and a happy stage, innocent time;

my best time that time in that old house, two windows up, a view over the river, where, summer nights, a carnival over the river you could hear the music and wish you were there, amid the bright lights in the dusk.

The carnival came in July. It had come in July as long as I could remember. And, nights, the lights, it was like Christmas in the summer. Standing by my window looking out. I remember how I felt, my childhood: the clothes that I wore, the progression of summers, the changing me, that carnival over the river. It is the earliest memory. A rare clarity. As yesterday. In a house with a cat, a wild one—it scratched me bloody. Darkie. I loathed that cat and it hated me. But we got along. Somehow. With my mother and father and older sister.

My father was big and thick-shouldered and with a tremendous chest. Balding a bit he blamed the army, the helmet he had worn. The cat was his, a strange joy; it sat on his knee while he flicked its ear. When he flicked its ear it blinked its eyes. Yellow. A slit of black. Night after night, flick and blink, until he died, the game went on.

He worked as a quarryman. In the country. Some place. I don't know where. But, an early riser, I never saw him in the mornings. A man who seldom smiled, not given to affection. Manly. He was easily the most manly man I have ever known. It is a lasting impression. He took a drink but gambled more. Horses were my father's passion. With the price of a pint he would opt for a bet. A worker, I never knew him sick or idle—in wintertime his hands were hacked, fingers and palms split open, wounds wide enough to stick your pinkie in—he always had his wages. Friday nights. There was a feeling in the house on Friday nights. My mother had the house cleaned. It sparkled. The waxcloth gleamed. The sink, a copper fount; the angle, long grace of a swan, positively shone. The fire blazed in the wall, cast on the window pane and you knew, the house, the clean cloth on the table, that it was Friday night. Pay night. My father gave me money, my pay. Sometimes I smelt beer on his breath, saw a glaze in his eyes, but just once I saw my father drunk, and a shocker that—like living with a madman, a violent stranger good for murder. It might be, the way drink took him, why he seldom drank.

My mother never drank. Few women then, there, other than bad, drank, or drank enough for it to show. The drinking game was strictly male.

Upstairs of our house was an uncle, Edward, a bachelor, who did drink. He drank like a fish. Weekly. Thursday (his pay night) to Saturday. Monday mornings he would beg his bus fare. Year after year, a pattern, Monday mornings, always nothing, he would beg his bus fare. Sometimes, too, the drink had him sick, too ill to work, to eat and I can remember my mother, his sister, nursing him—tea and toast, a bowl of soup—back to health, to fitness, too, in time, this would start all over again.

We all knew that it would, but nobody looked down on Edward. He was a single man, and, anyway, the Gorbals was full of drunkards, who, most of them, were accepted men. It was more the women who got the raw deal in that place. Visits to pawnshops. Stuff lifted on Fridays would go back in on Mondays, and, living there, it would have been easy to think that the world revolved on pubs and pawns.

It seemed, my childhood, first adolescence, that that place would never change, always be, the tenements ever stand. Cumberland Street. That was the street, the artery; most shops were there, pubs and pawns, and, on Wednesdays, a market in a lane. It was long, wooden-floored, with garish lights, a stale smell, and some of my first clothes—my father's jackets and working boots, were bought bargains from the hawkers. I remember how my mother haggled. You never paid the asking price. I thought it fun. I thought the chapel, St Francis, a pain. But I was made to go Sundays, First Communion and Saints days, sometimes the nights of the Stations of the Cross. My parents were religious. The priest had a lot of sway. It was an honour should he visit. These were my earliest years, the chapel in Cumberland Street, before, such cheer, as gala air, they built the chapel, St Bonaventure's, at the head of my own street. Opposite a rag store, across from a cinema, the Ritz, which was across from a pub, the Coronation.

About my street, which, the still tenement city, could have been just any street—I remember still each crack and dip. Short, alley-narrow, gas-lit, mean in summer—a terrible squalor—it could in winter, empty, rain or snow, gas mantles burning, be as homely as a postcard village. Seasons of the year. Time in my time. It was a long time home. Silverfir Street. I lived in a room and kitchen. All the houses there were room and kitchen or just a room, a kitchen, a single end—I knew families, ten or more, to have been raised in kitchens, single ends.

I was first aware of the street around the Coronation of 1952—the year that the chapel opened—when all the streets had parties. It was better than the carnival, banners and flags hanging; junk food and games and all for free. I won a race and got a prize, a pair of toy binoculars. The memory lingers. I see it yet. Some men got drunk, but the mood was good, no trouble, and one man, a pal's father, small but with the voice of a giant, he brought the place down with a rendering of 'Nellie Dean'.

It was a tough, hard street, but nothing was tougher, more enduring to me, than when I was twelve, the death of my father. I had thought him indestructible. That barrel-chested man. Blue-eyed. Fists like mallets. But he died, a heart attack, on a Saturday. November. Cold. I had played football in the morning. We played on a cinder pitch under a high red sun and coming home, on the street, if I was looked at I did not notice.

'Your father's dead,' my mother said, told me at the door.

Twelve years old, those were her very words and I never played football again.

I don't know why, what reason, I didn't play football again. For I was crazy about football. The shock should have gone, many a boy has lost his father and boys much closer to their fathers than I was to mine.

Whatever, he died and he was buried. What stuff he had my mother pawned; I lost his cat, so that no trace of him remained. Physical. But, God, how my mother pined. I thought she was going mad. And it was a bad time, a long time, her groanings in the mornings. My sister was little better. A sad, sad house. It got me down to shun it when I could. And that was I think what caused my trauma, stopped me playing football. A different mother and sister, I would have shrugged off the shock and lived my life—a different, better future.

But his death and their reaction, my age, nearing end of innocence, what innocence I had and now no or little discipline, I soon was running wild. Indeed I ran away. Made it down to Liverpool where, some notion to sail, to see the world, I wandered the docks just begging a ship. I begged too on the streets to eat. Two days I wandered Liverpool. Alone. Not giving a shit. In the end, though, I was picked up and sent home. My mother was no better. The house remained both sad and mad. I hated school, so no escape, for six months, a year, we all of us suffered and money so tight we all had to work. I went with milk. Mornings. Before school. Six till eight. Seven days. But I liked the job, the early rise, the still-sleeping city, and, no grief lasts forever, the house became a home again. At what cost to my head, my future, did the house become a home again? I have sometimes thought since my Liverpool adventure, that it would have been better had I gained a ship, departed Glasgow for a time. I have wondered too about my father, had he lived what might have been my future. It is hard, a stab in the dark, but I doubt my lot to drunkenness. As it was, a then fatherless child, unhappy house, rather than sport, the football, I had began to steal.

It was, stealing, in my class at school, a done thing. St Bonaventure's. A tough school. It long had the reputation of being a tough school and no class more tough than the class I was in. I would put odds on that, the toughness of that class, which was no good thing, one kid leading the next, till, in later years, three were up for murder, others murdered, and a good ten more in prison cells.

I got a couple of pounds for my work with the milk, that and tips. I kept the tips and gave my mother my pay. She had a job in school kitchens. My sister worked for an electric company. We got along. There was no need to steal. But with all or most of my classmates stealing, I followed suit. Why? I was not easily led, no one forced my arm, as later in my drinking years, no one fed me booze. No. It came round full circle, so that later to get my booze I had to steal. Sometimes. As at school I had to fight. Sometimes. But there was no excuse for my schoolboy stealing, or only the excuse of the place I lived, the kids I knew, a bit of respect and thrill in the night to burgle a shop. I burgled sometimes two or three shops in a night—walked strange streets to choose a target. Off the cuff. There was no planning. Just me and a couple of other kids tooled up looking for action. For a time, on dark winter nights, if no one was there, I would even go robbing alone.

Eventually, near to Christmas, this a year on from my father's death, I got caught. I got caught with another kid and they sent us, usual procedure, for a four day remand to a place called Larchgrove. I could go on, my time in there; I could, about the years till then, fill a volume, but suffice to say that the four days up I got probation. Two years. Thirteen to fifteen I was on probation. But it did not stop me robbing, I robbed even more recklessly than before, Christmas and all of the winter till, March or April, lightening nights, the phase—that all it was, a phase—died out.

I still (though almost sacked, my four days away) held down the milk job. But more sluggish now, I lacked the bounce I had when twelve. The early rise, no effort before, became a struggle. I was bleary-eyed in the mornings.

For sex was now the biggest thing, a terrible urge and I was badly in love with a girl named Nancy. Blonde. Blue-eyed. I had fancied her, her looks, from a long time back, the age of nine or ten. But it was innocent then, a cuddle at best, compared to what I wanted now. And I was hopeful—how she spoke, blinked to me, so much in love but hardly chaste, no faithful lover. Lust rode me as a white hot bar. All the time, and so suddenly sprung, as a thief in the night, it rode me. I ogled all the girls, Nancy's pals and sometimes, horseplay, was rewarded by a squeeze: feel of a tit. Till, a dark one, jet-black hair, late at night, alone with her, our tussle developed to more. Back of a close. She lay against me. No kidding then, a pliant weight. I felt her tits against my chest. Wind ruffled my hair. It felt cool on my belly and buttocks. But afterwards a queer shame. I could not look her in the eye. I wished with all my heart that nothing had happened, not with her. Two days after, no shame, more randy than ever, a prowling search, I sought her out.

I was fourteen when the booze felled Edward, the uncle upstairs.

What had happened, where he worked, a Government munitions, the place had closed and he was made redundant. There was severance pay, a couple of hundred, what had seemed a fortune then. Edward proceeded to blow it. What before was weekend drinking became a round the clock affair. I visited sometimes, took food to him, and there was always booze. Whisky and beer. Bottles littered his floor. The food went in the fire. Edward on a bender. And the more he drank the less he ate, till, after some weeks of it, he grew yellow and gaunt, sunken-eyed and it was no surprise that I heard him ill. In bed. I visited. He was lashed with sweat and a bucket filled with bile. The doctor was called for. I don't know what treatment, but the order was that he ceased to drink. Completely. A shandy was too much. The crisis passed. Edward gained his feet, his appetite. I thought him a nut, how he drank; the money he spent on stuff which made him sick. But off it then, and I should mention, the old tenements—the toilets were outside, on the stairs—were not the best of places to be convalescing.

The toilets of my close, one to a landing, three families, were especially grim. Long-narrow, black wet-walled, eight paces at least the door to the pan, no lighting, a floor that creaked, scuffle of rats—you first flushed the pan—and cold to freeze your balls. A visit there you made it quick, just in and out and you used a newspaper.

Edward recovered from that bout to drink again. Why? When he should have stopped, had been told, the price of his health, his life, to stop.

I visited him still, but he was failing. I saw him failing, fourteen years old I saw what drink could do. In his house and on the street. It was worse when you saw him on the street—the fear that he would fall. A particular day, noon, Edward drinking from morning, he must have been drinking from morning, I, from my window, saw him fall. He was outside the pub, the Railway Tavern, where he had been drinking. A summer day, hot, the sun struck down, bounced off the street and Edward, who, swaying in a dark suit, white shirt, seemed to straighten up—as if to gain full height for a spectacular pitch.

I, two storeys high, through glass, heard the crack his head made on stone. It hurt *my* head and why did he do this to himself?

When I gained the street, a record time, two men had Edward standing up. Dazed. Swaying. Dripping blood. The blood dripped from his chin to splash his shoes. Edward as a redskin. Wet. The blood like paint, a shirt once white now scarlet.

Between us, the men and I, we hustled Edward over the

street. Some people now watched, women and kids. Edward out, slack, a dead weight, it was like humping a corpse. Which, his pitch, now tumbling blood, it crossed my mind he might soon be. The blood, it sheeted down, alarmed me. I had seen guys cut, face-hit with knives, but nothing like this. We all of us, all four, were painted. Carrying Edward up the stairs. Spiral. When we got him to bed I fled the house. Left the men, two strangers, with my wounded uncle. For I was sick of him, his blood and I could not eat that lunchtime. Washing my hands, cleaning my shoes—and why was I stuck with a man like Edward?

As things turned out I was not to be stuck with him much longer. That day, I'm sure, his burst head was the beginning of the end for him. Edward died in the winter of the same year, 1958.

At school, an unholy place if Catholic, a small education— my whole time there, three years, I know I learned nothing, or nothing academic—there was some drinking in the toilets. Cheap wine. Red. But I didn't partake, stayed clear of the toilets—smokey holes, stale—a smell of piss depressed me.

So I stayed out, away from the wine, and away from the boys who drank it. They were the wild ones, wild sober, crazy drunk, glazed-eyed, swaggering, toying with knives and if not afraid I was not stupid. I'd fight if I had to, but aspired to be no hardman. I don't know what I aspired to, but it wasn't that, a place full of hardmen what was another?

Anyway I was something of a loner, lone-wolf then, and what pals I had were not at school. And at fourteen years old I was seldom at school. It was easy to dodge. The teachers seemed not to care. Just now and again you had to go, keep the school-board from the door. My final year, I spent more time in the cinema (*The Ten Commandments, The Vikings*, come to mind) than I did in class.

I was pally then with a couple of guys who worked with me on the milk. They were older, full-time workers, sixteen, seventeen years old with a noon-time stop, so I was not lonely on my visits to the movies.

But those two or three years, fourteen to sixteen, seventeen, there is a mighty difference, and I did not, not then, go with them nights.

Nights I hung with a different crowd, where Nancy was, for I was still in love with that blonde who knew, who teased me—she was a natural flirt—but it was fun I guess, first puppy love, street corners, under gas-light, and a fine feeling then how I felt for Nancy.

At home, my behaviour—little schooling, late nights: I was out most nights till early morning—worried my mother and there were rows and I got mad. Mad I think that I loved her so. A love different from my love for Nancy. I did not want to hurt her. Yet to live my life I had to hurt her. I was no more a little boy, my feelings, stirring manhood, and it is not good at that age for a boy to live in a female house however well-intended. Their, my mother and sister, wish was to protect when all they did was smother and cause rows, until, not long after I could take no more and hit the road. I would I know, regardless of what happened, if nothing had happened, have hit the road.

It was around this time that the Gorbals began to vanish. Demolition squads seemed everywhere. And the people moving out. They, most of them, the ones I knew, moved to Castlemilk, a huge housing scheme; and already half of the kids at school lived there. Houses with hot water and inside toilets. I remember a first bath there, at a pal's house.

My mother, this change, the Gorbals tumbling down, had her name on the list for a house in Castlemilk. But I doubt that she was crazy to shift to leave the street and the people she knew. As for myself, I didn't care—anywhere where Nancy was was fine with me. But I was beginning to hear stories about her. And once, a kid with a squint, I beat him up for his talk about Nancy. Secret love? I wonder. I think that all the kids, the boy with the squint, and Nancy and her brother knew.

The brother was younger by a couple of years but had the same good looks and he began to hang around me.

At first I had hardly noticed him, then suddenly—I think it was the way he smiled—I found myself in an odd position.

Strangely, at this time, I still went to chapel on Sundays. I went to sit and kneel but I did not pray. I was done with praying—you might pray all day and still have a hard—on.

But the shape I was in, in torment—I was riddled with guilt-I began again to pray. I prayed to be done with the brother, the hold he had on me and wished now that I had never met the both of them.

But did I? For the brother was there, in the chapel, an altar boy, on the red carpet, sweet in light and dressed in white. His head fairly glowed, golden strands to dim the chalice and mock my prayers. Was I a fraud in the balcony? It puzzles me yet. For pray I did to break the chains, a growing attraction, and worse, what bugged me most, affection.

The kid for all his looks, or because of them, a fragile beauty, as flower in bloom, was at odds in that place, those tenements, unlike his sister who flourished there.

I ponder here for it is hard, so screwed-up were my feelings then; as manhood threatened, or so it seemed, in that chapel, an adoring eye on the altar boy, cause of my fall, while I prayed for redemption. Little wonder that I prayed in vain. A case for the nuthouse or a suffering saint.

It got that I would wait for him outside, though not I hoped that he would know the cause of my standing there. It was with terrible shame, ache in my heart, that I waited for that altar boy. At first. Time went on I didn't care, and mid-week too, Evening Devotions, I would wait for him. As I was always there, hanging around the chapel; it brought the attention of the priest, who, old, Irish, thought I had a

calling: 'Sure, and it's the grand life, Michael, the work of
God.'

I eased up a bit on my visits then, following the shock of
that, soon stopping them altogether.

The brother asked me why, what was the matter or reason
for my non-attendance.

'I'm fed up with it.'

'You liked it before.'

'You think that I liked it before.'

'You never?'

'I don't know.' Walking with him. 'You believe all that
stuff?' The top of his head reached to the bridge of my nose.
'But you look good on the altar.'

'You think?' He was not reticent, anything but. 'It was
how you came, me on the altar?' Smiling. So like his sister,
blue-eyed smiling. Sometimes he was awful like Nancy, at
the eyes, the flare of his nose. But lighter, smaller, younger.
A boy, not girl and that was my problem or delight.

'It was,' he said, a smile, all the tease of his sister. 'I think.'

'But I don't come now.'

'Naw,' he said. Then, 'How don't you come now?'

'I told you, I was fed up with it.'

'With me?'

'You're a strange kid.'

'But you still like me?'

'Sure I still like you.'

We walked alongside of a graveyard wall. The road was
wide, long, dead flat. I walked on the outside, he in to the
wall.

'But,' he said, 'you like Nancy tae.'

'She's okay.'

'She's a ride,' he said.

The whole crumbling place was tumbling, crumbling
down.

'Aw the guys, they've aw been up her.'

I said nothing.

'Hiv you?'

'Naw.'

'Then aw the guys except for you.'

I felt a choke in my throat—'*Aw the guys, they've aw been up her.*'

'She's just,' he said, 'a dirty cow.'

We walked a bit.

'Is it,' he asked, 'how you go with me?'

'How'd you mean,' I was embarrassed, 'go with you?'

'Aw,' he said, 'forget it.'

'You think tae get Nancy I go with you?'

'I don't know how I mean.'

'We're pals,' I said.

'Sure.' But how he said it, flippant, surly, looking down.

'You want tae be pals?' I asked him.

'I don't know what I want.' Still looking down, a darkened head, slender shoulders, the white of his neck and something, a loneliness, both his and mine, I laid my hand upon his shoulder. It was the first time I had ever touched him. He tensed, shuddered. I felt his shudder, a vibration in my fingers.

We stopped. Stood. He looked at me. His face was pasty, eyes dark, big and liquid. In the night. Standing. Tears glistened on his cheeks. I touched his face. Right or wrong, touching him, his face, I did not care. Not then, not after and after it was not his face alone I touched.

That was winter, near to Christmas in 1958. I turned fifteen in February, 1959. Out of school, officially, later that year I got a job with a music publisher. Two days there and I hated it more than I had hated school, which was something.

The boss was a stocky, little, Jewish guy, who as they say, liked his pound of flesh. My position there was as a message boy and the trouble was, as opposed to school, where there was nothing to lose, if you didn't go, you got no pay. For all that was. A miserly sum. I gave it to my mother. Un-opened. A brown envelope. But even so, the milk job with tips and pay earned me more for myself.

There was just one boy—a religious sort—he carried a bible and we, along with the boss, were the only males there. The girls, there were about eight of them, ranged from prissy to bold together with a typist who, a dame around thirty, went to Spain on holiday. I was impressed: most people I knew went to Dunoon or Largs, if they went on holiday.

You started at nine and finished at six. I brushed the place and tramped the streets, delivered sheet-music to shops in the city centre. At night I went with the mail. Two or three times each night I went with the mail, more sheet-music, cylinder-wrapped, and it chanced one night that a woman was robbed. She was old and bent and could hardly see. I saw her but she did not see me. In the Post Office. I followed her out. By chance I followed her out. The street was short, a pawn and a pub, and, save for the woman, who tapped with a stick, was empty as I walked it.

Back in the shop they had more mail stacked. You worked that place for what money you got. So I had another load and was ready to go when two cops, plainclothes men—I knew one and he knew me—walked in.

It was a Friday night, I had my pay in my pocket, the July carnival was over the river and the cop came over—such a show as if I was fucking Dillinger. 'You followed her out.'

The boss, the little Jewish guy, was listening.

'Why'd you dae it, the cop asked me, 'rob the poor auld wumin?'

I was heading for a trip to jail when a new cop, uniformed, appeared to tell that the thief was caught. He was a guy around fifty, nothing like me.

I had forgotten the thing when, Monday morning, I was sacked. On the spot. A week's pay in lieu. I was too sickened to protest, to say a word.

My first job. I had worked two months. Walking home,

I felt so small, and I hated Jews—I had never liked cops—for a long time after.

It was that summer I got a first new suit and first went dancing. To the Dennistoun Pallie. A Monday or Wednesday night. With Willie and Rab, the guys who worked with me on the milk. The suit was Italian style, whatever that meant, but the in thing then, and I felt very smart with bright coloured socks and pointed shoes and we went for a drink before we went dancing.

I did not want the drink, but it seemed to be the thing to do, and a certain glamour to stand at the bar. We each bought a round, heavy beer, foul-tasting stuff to my virgin gut. The pub was big and noisy, full of kids going dancing and a merry air, atmosphere. I liked the atmosphere if I disliked the beer, the cost of the stuff—it was not cheap.

When we got to the dancing, a place big as a barn, I was a little drunk, light-headed.

The girls stood back from the boys, against a wall. I had begun to smoke then and smoked and looked and felt a glow of well-being. Three pints of heavy beer. They now worked a treat, wormed my head, I thought to stand two inches taller. In my Italian suit, pointed shoes, viewing the ladies, who, in the light of the place, how I felt, showed better than they were.

The place was crushed, hot and sticky in the summer night. You had to push to move. I was a bit disappointed that there were more boys than girls, who, a lot of them, refused to dance. Willie and Rab had a hard time trying to get a girl to dance. I was content to just watch, listen to the music. Slow. They danced to records. Amplified. Songs of love. The dance floor was thick with couples, dancing close, the ones I watched danced very close—cheek to cheek with bellies pressing. I thought it sexy and worth the price, the entrance charge, just watching them, listening to the music.

At first. Then, a tap on my shoulder, I turned to see Nancy. Standing. Smiling. Good teeth, blue eyes. In a low-cut dress. She had startled me but not too much, the wonder of the booze, three pints of heavy beer. It had a beguiling effect. I was glad to see her, I always was, but this time was a bit different, as she seemed glad to see me. And, again the beer, magic stuff, I told her that she looked a treat: 'But I can't dance.'

'It's easy,' she said. 'It's slow.'

So we danced, you could call it that, for who led who I do not know, but this was the first time that I had held her, and the record, Johnny Mathis, 'Twelfth of Never'—all in all it was quite a night.

I saw her home. She wore a red coat with a fur collar. And looking snug, chic in it, I could hardly believe my luck.

Luck?

I much preferred her brother, felt more for him than I did for her—I felt nothing for her once I had my way, but, this is how such things go—or how they went for me in my crooked trip—not wanting her, she wanted me.

I then had a job in an animal-food joint. The pay was good and I had quit on the milk. Worked just eight till four, five days; a different set-up, more free than with the music publisher. But you still had to work, and worked as cheap labour, performed a man's task for cut wages, a boy's stamp. My first two jobs, two Shylocks. That age is when you miss a father most. I had an interest in wood, the work of a carpenter, but an apprenticeship, five years of it, the pay was too small. So I shovelled animal feed: old biscuits, dud fruit, a lot of shit, for ultimately, fattened beasts, the knacker's yard.

There were about six other boys worked with me there. In a shed in a lane, and the owner's son was foreman. A long-jawed beanpole the kids called Stick. But not a bad

boss, he left you alone. Why not? The work got done. If the
work hadn't got done there'd have been none of us there.
You got hired in that place on the strength of your back.
Temporarily. You turned eighteen, a man, a bigger insurance stamp, you got the sack. The rules were simple in that
dead-end hole.

Still I liked or did not mind it for a time. The guys were
cheery, ragamuffin, rough and ready, and one of them—he
had just one eye—I already knew. We, this kid and I, every
pay day, got in the habit of a lunchtime drink. There was a
pub at the corner, a dive which sold wine, cheap cider,
where, the idea I think to prove myself a man, I would
swallow a few. Lunchtime. Pints of beer. At night I might
have a couple more. Pay day. I drank at no other time and
still grudged the money, the price of the beer.

But by this nippling at it I was sure to fall. I know now
that I was sure to fall, get good and drunk. Sooner or later
and it turned out sooner, before my sixteenth year. It came
unexpectedly, with a bang, a Saturday night, in a pub called
the Pig and Whistle.

Like many another I had met with a pal. I doubt any
drunkard first drank alone. And passing the pub, a corner
shop, McNeil Street, just up from the Clyde, I had no
intention of drinking.

It was autumn, late September or October, shades of night
and a fine rain falling. I wore my Italian suit. There was a
cafe at the end of the street and it was there that I was going.

Until I met the pal, who was not really a pal—he was too
old for that, to be a pal. I'd just seen him around, at the
corners, but, whatever, what talk, a quick one, we went for
a drink. In the Pig and Whistle. A long straight bar, dark
polished wood. We drank Newcastle ale from pint bottles.
It was my first shift away from heavy beer. My pal (I'll call
him that) showed me how to pour, to tip the glass to get a
head. He had big hands, big dirty nails, and his talk was all
of fighting. The more we drank the more he talked of

fighting. I remember that. I remember too, a year or so after, a fight, street brawl, that he was dead. In the gutter. My tutor. Guy showed me to pour ale.

At first when we entered the bar was half empty and the barman queried my age: 'We've got tae ask.'

I told him eighteen, the legal limit, and that was that, no further questions. But standing by that bar, I, my reflection in the gantry mirror, just a kid, a boy, I looked no more than my proper age. Fifteen. I remember that too, my reflection in the gantry mirror, for, that place, the men around, I wished that I looked older.

A few drinks in and I didn't care, nor could I see to care: those Newcastle's packed a jolt.

How things went, my pal met pals till there were about ten of us and the booze came fast and furious. I thought to go but again thought to stay, match these people glass for glass.

Whisky appeared. I drank it raw. It seared my throat, burned my gut and there seemed to be no end to it, the whisky, for each glass I drank there was another waiting. I grued at the stuff but drank it down. The price to be a man. The fellows I drank with were all in their twenties. I felt somehow to prove myself. I don't know why. Or it might have been my affair with the brother, but I do not think it was my affair with the brother.

I have no idea how long I stayed, lingered there, but in a fight of sorts some punches were flung and I got hit in the eye. I remember that. Still nothing serious, the fight or my eye, we were soon all back drinking, pals again.

The next I remember I was locked in the loo, on my knees, my Italian suit, bent over the pan. Sweat dripped from my brow, a rollicking vomit, the whole place swinging, and that, my head in the pan, a roaring in my ears, is the last I remember of that night.

I awoke with a lurch, a bursting head, throbbing eye. I slept in a recess bed in the kitchen. The curtain was drawn but I knew that it was late, my mother and sister talking. I felt still sick, a queasy gut, and was sore across my chest which felt hollow and wracked from the violence of my vomit. Remorse? I don't know that I felt remorse. I felt too bad, the pain in my chest, my injured eye, to feel remorse. In that bed, where, a child, I had suffered from measles and whooping cough, but nothing like this—both physical hurt and missing time, lost memory.

It was an agony to raise my head. There was blood on my shirt-front, my hands. I tried to remember but couldn't remember. I remembered the whisky and wanted to puke. I would have stayed in bed but was needing a piss, a drink. I was terribly dry, and that, after all I had drank, struck me as odd.

Nobody spoke about my appearance from the curtain. My mother and sister just looking, and looking hurt. Prissy. I crossed to the sink, a drink, cold water, before my piss. I still wore my clothes from the night before. A night I wished I had never seen. It was no use talking, I felt too ill for any talk and after my piss I went back to bed, a bombed-out sleep.

I awoke again in the middle of the night with a raging hunger. My head still hurt but my belly ached more. I washed a bit and heated some meat, the dinner from the day before. It was not enough. I was never so hungry. I wolfed down bread and cheese, a pint of milk, all the food that I could find. A banquet in the night. It got me feeling better, more able, fitter to assess the damage. My eye was moused and a cut on my forehead. I fancied, the cut on my forehead, my brush with the pan. That seemed funny now, what before had loomed a horror. But what had happened after? I had no memory. Nothing. My head was a total blank, and that was frightening. I would have rathered a physical hurt, what I could understand, explain, than what I could not. The thing was scary. I decided to forget it, or try to forget it; in time I had forgotten.

I smoked. Cigarettes I did not usually smoke, could not remember buying. The house was quiet and all the other house windows were blacked out, curtained over, it seemed that I alone was awake in the city. It was both lonely and peaceful, looking over my clothes, rumpled and stained, splashed blood and vomit. My Italian suit, I had been so proud of that suit, fussy—mothballs, in the pockets—like a woman for its care. Now reduced to this, a hobo garb. I went through the pockets thinking to have it cleaned. There was still some money, copper and silver, six shillings or so to last me through till pay day.

I thought of the ale, the bottles of Newcastle and I blamed the whisky. I shuddered at the thought of the whisky. Rot-gut stuff had stole my head. I would drink it no more. I could see no sense, the sickness, the money you spent, in drinking whisky. Beer, a long drink, cool, was one thing, whisky quite another. I would drink it no more, not that or Newcastle's, but stick to heavy beer, stuff which gave me a lift without the sickness.

So I thought. A wasted Sunday. I had slept all through the Sunday. I drank some tea and went back to bed, now impatient for the morning.

At work I got in a fight, a special one, for my opponent, a boxer, had won some things, medals and cups, and, once, after a win, had his photo in the paper.

He was shorter, but wider, more heavy than I. I was growing all-shot then, all arms and legs, too big feet with a baby face. He had a wise-guy look, a flattened nose, some eyebrow scars. 'Strong as a bull,' they said he was. He looked it. I saw it, how he lifted heavy weights. And the bastard thing about fighting him, after just a few bad words, insults flung, was I liked the guy.

But the fight was fixed. Lunchtime. We would neither of us back down. That place, those guys, you just couldn't back down and stay in the job. They would make your stay a misery.

We fought on a floor of oats. He came in on me with a boxer's stance, a shuffle, working his mouth, his lips. The kids ringed around us, even Stick who, so long as it was lunchtime, liked a fight.

My belly pulsed. The boxer looked tough. Some hair on his chest. Compact. I knew nothing of boxing, of this kind of fight. Guys I'd fought it was an instant thing, they came in mad, wide-open, looking to kill you in their rage. This was my first fixed fight, a time and place, bare-chested, and I felt a little stupid, naked, as we both of us circled in the circling circle.

Then, a blink, I was hit. Hard. On the mouth. The punch slammed back my head, slackened my teeth. I could feel the front ones swing. There was nothing stupid then, just blood on my chin and a roar in my head and wanting to kill the bastard. But the punches I threw wound round his neck or over his head and I could not catch him clean. At the same time he dug to my body with shots over my kidneys, my hanging ribs. The pain was so fierce that I almost screamed. I tried to clinch, hold back his arms, trip him down. But nimble with a surprising strength, he shook me away. Easily. I wished for clothes that I might get a hold, that he was taller that I might try for a butt. This was not my kind of fight. The guy was slippery as an eel, in and out, his hammering fists. I heard them slam against my sides, was rocked back when they crashed my temples. I had no idea a man, a fist, could hit so hard. And no escape, I couldn't run—when beaten back the circle pushed me forward.

It was no contest. He was too heavy, too strong, two years too old.

Still I split his eye, had him bloody and was still on my feet when Stick stopped the fight. Some pride in that, the punches I'd taken, I was still on my feet, still willing to trade and fight on; Stick stopped the massacre.

I mention that fight, give details, for the boxer became a pal—he became a professional too—and I tried my hand at boxing.

The boxer encouraged me, and I went with him to a gym in Dennistoun, near to the Pallie, where a whole bunch of kids worked out. I liked it straight off, the sounds, smells, and it seemed I possessed a natural flair. One thing was certain, I could take a punch. It was a good time, that gym and I was full of boxing, great fighters, champions were my men then. I read about them all I could, how they trained and a whole new language, hooks and jabs, jabbing off of the hook, bolo punching, and I learned the story of Benny Lynch, world's flyweight champion, a Gorbals' boy—who could beat the best but could not beat the bottle.

I met men who had known Lynch and who spoke of his drinking as much as his boxing, and—he had been buried in a pauper's grave—I thought the guy a fucking fool, that he had thrown it all away.

I went to the gym three nights a week and each session grew a little better, stronger—and boxing is the best way I know of, if you want to make a boy into a man, to change him for the better.

My mother saw my change—and the change was dramatic—I was early to bed and early to rise, a run before work—she thought her prayers had been answered.

But again at my age, my father was missed. If my father had been alive I would, I'm sure, I have no doubt, have tangled a boxer for many a year. Fate. It was not to be, and if I tangled a boxer for three months I was lucky. But the happiest three months, something I liked, did good, in a place I was accepted, fitted.

'I'm pregnant.'
'You're kidding.'
'I'm not.'
'You're sure?'
'The doctor told me.'
'When?'
'Yesterday.'
'You think it was me?'
'I *know* it was you.'
'I don't think it was me.'
'You kin take a test.'
'Test?'
'Blood test.'
'It proves something?'
'It'll prove that it was you.'
'You've told your mother?'
'It was her that took me tae the doctor.'
'Why d'you not say before?'
'I didn't know before.'
'I still don't think that it was me.'
'I expected it tae be like this.'
'Like what?'
'You bastard.'
I smiled, it was all I could do.
'My mammy, she's going round tae see your mammy.'
'*When's* your mammy going round tae see my mammy?'
'Tonight,' Nancy said. 'She's going round tonight.'
Standing at the corner. Winter. I was nudging sixteen. Nancy. She was sixteen. I wondered, and not for the first time, in two ruined years, whatever I had seen in her. Indeed, her mammy meeting my mammy, I could have run away right there and then. At the corner. Beside a shop. I bought cigarettes. A first smoke in months. I have been smoking ever since. I am smoking now.

My mother asked me was it true.

I hung my head.

My sister called me stupid.

I felt stupid.

'You might be stuck with her,' she said.

In the kitchen, around the fire, me smoking, thinking, but knowing, not if I lived for a hundred years would I ever live with Nancy. I had the thing in my head that she had tricked me somehow. Like girls, those things, knew better than boys. Everyone knew girls knew those things better than boys. Nancy's problem was she didn't know me, not quite. I would up and go, it was as simple as that, make my way in London.

I had thought before of going to London and before the boxing had almost gone, lit-out, to a place they said was paved with gold.

'It's your decision,' my mother said.

'We'll see,' I said. But I think we all of us knew that I was going, it was the best excuse I'd ever have.

I met with the brother—I saw a lot of the brother.

'It's true?' he asked.

I smiled. Shrugged. It was all I could do. I still liked him.

'I told you that she was a cow.'

Never did a brother have such spite for a sister as that boy then. 'I warned you,' he said.

'I know.'

'You're getting hitched?'

'I'm a bit young for getting hitched.'

'She thinks you will.'

I said nothing.

'Nancy,' he said, he was no fool, 'she'll soon find herself another mug.'

I missed that kid, I missed the boxing—but I had to go. Even with no hassle, no thing with Nancy, I would have gone to London.

I had a drink, got mildly drunk the night I went. With Willie and Rab, the boxer and the one-eyed guy. In a pub in Argyle Street under the Central Station bridge. On beer I got mildly drunk. I remembered too well the whisky and ale, my night in the Pig and Whistle. But a merry night and, for me, the start of a great adventure. London. I had long thought about it, a city of light, where the action was, as a kid from Seattle might think of New York.

I departed Glasgow in January of 1960. I forget the date but it was a Friday. I was a month short of my sixteenth year. The decade was to be a hummer. You could feel it in the air. Rebellion. Kids of the war and the post-war years. I was an early starter. Too early. London was yet to swing. Still was staid. A pot of hypocrisy. The painted face and dirty drawers. I hit the joint two years too soon.

What struck me first was the immigrants working in the station. Euston. Every second guy seemed black. To me. I who had seen few blacks or Asians. The great invasion was yet to come, flood Scotland.

Out of the station a soft rain fell. The day was grey, as dusk and over the river, so many bridges, the traffic was all lit up. I wandered the heart of the place looking for Piccadilly. And a big disappointment that there was no circus, canvas tent. My looking for a circus, and I looked a long time for the tent, should serve to show how green I was in that place, how I saw it, see it still, where no whore can compete with a fresh young boy. So if I missed on the circus I found a Sodom. Was eyed as a girl. I got the hell away from Piccadilly. Where, had I chose, I could have sold my arse but could not buy drink.

I tried to buy booze. A couple of pubs—mild beer or bitter, but they kicked me out. The rain continued all that day. Saturday. I met with a hunchback in a cafe: hot pies and beans, cracked cups—I had a couple of helpings—and the hunchback got me lodgings.

His name was Anton, the first pal I made in London. A clockmaker who came from Prague. Where, so he said, he was a famous clockmaker. Certainly his room was full of clocks—you could hardly move for clocks—but the weird thing about that room, hundreds of clocks, it was silent as the tomb.

I stayed in the room below Anton who stayed below a warlock, a tall thin guy with long black hair and a sickly pallor, who, eventually, though I seldom saw him, was taken to the madhouse, a joy to Anton, who was scared of him.

That was later. Saturday night Anton and I drank wine. Cheap plonk. Red. He did not think I was too young. We sat amongst the litter of clocks, a ginger cat and I thought it high adventure. The hunchback, truly his was a whopper hump, as though his head sat on his belly, the clocks and cat and the bottles of plonk. My first night in London. The mist had cleared but the rain still filtered, the softest drizzle and I wondered how it was, rain or sleet or an ice-hard night in Glasgow.

Monday morning I got a job. It was no problem to get a job in London as opposed to Glasgow where you had to hunt. The first place I asked, an oatmeal factory, I got started and started within the hour. The work was lighter and the pay better than in the beast-feed place. I worked nine to five, five days, got paid Thursdays and in a week or so I had made some pals, kids my own age. We used to meet in cafes, hang around, feel up the girls (I had my eye on a dusky one, Katie, a look-alike for Shirley Bassey, how Shirley Bassey looked at that time), and I liked London, the East End, the Cockneys that I palled with, nights in the cafes, the juke box music, the girl who looked like Shirley Bassey.

There was of course a more shady side, a billiard parlour, gangster brothers, where the scene was like Chicago. They were dark, tough-looking men, the brothers Kray. I went a couple of times, at night, for a bit of a thrill, as an air of expectation, a visit to that billiard parlour.

But in London as Glasgow, time wore on, in a couple of months, the age I was, some booze crept in. There were pubs that would serve us: in the East End there were a lot of pubs that would serve us. Overnight we shifted out from the cafes to pubs. It seemed as if it were overnight, that my troubles started.

I had till then sent money home. Weekly. Thursdays. Out of my pay packet. But now nights in pubs, some pints, a game of darts or dominoes, it was impossible to send money home. I felt guilty about it, it spoiled my drinking, nights in the pubs—better pubs, bigger, more jolly, than the Glasgow ones. But so expensive. For a night in a pub you could have a week in a cafe. But suddenly the cafes were out. We all wanted to go to the pub, and, in truth, I liked the beer, the atmosphere. So to get more money I changed my job, but even that, outdoor work, was not enough.

I thought, first time in London and first time for gain, to go out robbing. But luck found an easier way in the person of Anton who presented a gift. I was by then very pally, the only pal of Anton, who would buy me beer, some bottles—I disliked the wine—and late at night, the room full of clocks, the ginger cat, assorted junk, we would sit and talk.

I told him about Glasgow, my affair with Nancy, how I had to flee that city. He understood, an affair of the heart and we talked of many things, his childhood in Prague, the good years, a prosperous Anton, tender of church bells, the clock towers of Prague, before the war—a war, Hitler's armies, had ruined it all.

'They hated hunchbacks.'

For a time Anton hid in a belfry.

I thought it a wonderful story.

But more, speaking with him, him on the wine, sometimes crying, the good years in Prague, or bad—hiding in the belfry—I spied mid the junk, the litter of clocks, brass candlesticks. They were easy to steal—my first theft for drink, although at the time, I did not think of it being for drink. There was a ready market for candlesticks and also clocks as I discovered.

I first felt a snake after robbing from Anton, but not too long and not too bad a snake. He was old and I was young, and it was not like stealing money. I consoled myself that it was not like stealing money, with so many clocks, what were a few? I chose at random. Anton spoke of his days in Prague. I became a regular in the antique shops, no questions asked and they chiselled me good out of the old man's treasure.

Still, with what money I got, a substantial amount, I was able to treat in pubs, buy new clothes and a motor scooter and Anton never knew.

Even then, sixteen years old, I was drinking far too much. I thought it manly. It cheered me, rid me of my troubles, inhibitions, I had a near crippling shyness, and so helped me with the girls. Also I took pride in the amount that I could drink. Other kids, men even—the road gang that I worked with—when they collapsed I smiled on indulgently.

At times I thought of the boxing, how, though smoking and drinking now, I missed it. I thought of joining a London club, but at night, the pubs were so much nearer.

So what chance I had as a boxer I blew, and I still regret the boxing.

But the trick, the trap of booze—when full of it I felt no guilt or regrets. Not about nothing, the boxing or the hunchback's clocks, the money I spent or how I behaved. And I behaved as no angel. I have still the scars, jumbled knuckles of fights, of a night when I punched in each car windscreen that I saw. And that was just on beer, no spirits or wine, horrors of the things to come, I wrote off for youth, high spirits. Out of work, almost in jail, near loss of a

finger—I still have the scar to remind me how I almost lost
my finger.

Summer in London, I can see myself—I need no photo—tall,
already six foot, but wafer-thin. The guys called me Stick. I
shifted my drink from beer to stout, hoping to beef-up. I was
scared to weigh myself, a fear of cancer—such a skin of
bones, some gristle. Another problem with this shooting up,
dropping weight, my clothes were always short in the arms
and legs, so that I felt sometimes like a seaside clown. And
I hated the nickname. Stick. It reminded me somehow,
Glasgow slang, of a whoremaster—a stickman. And the
other Stick, the boss's son, the beast-feed place, I'd detested
him. There was nothing I liked in the nickname, but we all,
or most of us, had nicknames and I had to bear with it.

This thinness, no butt worth the mention, straight up and
down, near drove me crazy. I couldn't understand it. The
more I ate and I ate like a horse, drank gallons of stout, the
more skinny I got. I worried that cancer was eating me up
and thought to see a local doctor, who turned out to be gay.

Young, not thirty, not bad–looking, he smiled as I told
him my fear.

'My dear boy.'

I was dubious, the guy—his smile, and up on his couch,
his ear to my chest, my thumping heart, I had quite a surprise
from that medical man.

When it was over he pronounced me fit.

I looked at him.

He looked at me.

I asked him for a tonic.

'Whatever for?'

'Tae fatten me up.'

'But it's just your age, a wonderful age.'

And it was a wonderful morning leaving him. Cleansed.
Free of a cancer I never had. But a little shaken by his

attention, it's not every doctor who pays you. I went for a drink.

I had some beer then ordered a whisky. On the spur of the moment I ordered the whisky. Why? I'll never know why. The bar was long and curved and dark. You stood on a carpet. Brown or red or red turned brown. I drank the whisky for all it was, a minute drop, a swallow.

Next I was talking to a Welshman, a short, thick guy from Cardiff. He was down on his luck in the dress of a tramp. I treated: more whisky and beer and I think I gave him money. It would have been my way to give him money. But the day is hazed and I can't be sure; and I don't remember leaving him or that pub.

I awoke in jail, a white tiled cell with a twist of stitches over my eye. The pain in my eye had awoken me. Without the pain I would have slept much longer. I wished to have slept much longer. The mystery of this cell, my hospital visit—I had wits enough to know that I must have been to hospital—was one almighty fright.

What the fuck had happened?

I shuffled round the cell, a big brown door, feeling thoroughly wretched, a hurting head, throbbing eye, and there was nothing big, manly, about drunkenness now. No. And for the first time in London I felt homesick. Very young. Vulnerable. I wanted to go home. See my mother and sister, the people I knew, had known since a child. A first nostalgia, the booze still in me, I sat down and wept. I wept though my back was to the door, the Judas hole, not wishing the keepers to see my weakness. It was the first time since a kid, short pants, a tantrum, I had wept. I was what I was in that cell, a boy and a boy with a problem even then.

My tears had dried when they let me go. There was no one saw me weep. I acted tough. Swaggered. Smiled. I was to swagger and smile a whole lot of my life, for days, inside, I was cracking up, something so near and yet so far.

I got out, I think, on a two pound bail. Forfeited. Which meant I need not appear in court, a charge of drunkenness— I had fallen, it seemed, and burst my eye.

It was still light, the pubs were still open, when they let me go. I remember a red-shot sky. The night was warm. Balmy. And still drunk, or none too sober; but feeling rotten, I made my way to the nearest pub—one I knew would serve me.

A curer. A hair of the dog. I had heard about it, and how I felt that red-shot night, the city of London, the pain in my eye, it seemed to be the thing to do. Truly. For whatever else, it could make me feel no worse.

I found a pub and ordered beer. A pint, then six; it was a wonder how I drank that beer. Near a pint in each swallow. I had no taste for whisky. I would never drink whisky again. And again thinking to go home, pack up and leave this place, a pack of lies the stories I'd heard had been told about it. There were no streets of gold, or what gold you got you had to work for, hump sacks or dig those streets to get.

A well of self-pity came of my time in jail, the shame that I had wept, flooded hot tears that I couldn't avoid. Had anyone seen my tears I would have departed London then and there. That I know, for my pride was huge, at least what I took for pride was huge.

A blue, queer mood came over me drinking my beer, debating to go home.

But thinking of my eye, the stitches, it seemed better to stay till I got them out.

Shifting thoughts. I smoked. I thought of the boxing and thought to return. I thought the beer a magic brew—my second drink, near drunk alone—how good it would be to return, go home a champion. I saw it in that pub, my return as champion; a tailored dark suit, dark glasses.

My mood, the thought, the beer, swung from blue to jolly to a positive high.

I felt good.

There were guys I knew, hung around with in the pub. I kidded, when they asked about my eye, that I had been mugged: 'But they never got nothing.'

It ended, the night, a whole group of us, and drunk again—as drunk as I'd been—someone took me home.

I think that someone took me home.

That summer: long hot nights, blue-sky days, no unemployment (you wanted work you got work), we most of us had motor scooters. Vespa or Lambretta; I think a couple of other makes too, but the main ones were Vespa or Lambretta. Mine was red, a Vespa, a big fraud aerial and bright with flags. I rode it drunk or sober or high on dope—sometimes, some of the kids, they had some pills or hashish—and at weekends a whole gang of us would ride down to the coast, to Brighton or Margate.

There were always girls on those trips, pillion passengers, and we would drink in the pubs and screw on the beaches.

I had still a passion, attraction, all this time for Katie the girl (Irish mother, West Indian father) who looked like Shirley Bassey. But she seemed cosseted by a tribe of brothers, all tough young men, like a gang on their own. So I could but look, admire her, lithe and smooth, coffee, just a kink or curl in her blue-black tresses.

But again, as with Nancy and Nancy's brother, a rare shyness—a fear of rejection—it was not the brothers that deterred me. I didn't give a hoot for the brothers. Her rejection, a girl still at school, not yet fifteen, was more what bothered me.

I saw Katie in the cafes, street corners at night, I made a point to see her there, trying to be casual, sidling up to sit or stand beside her. It was, or almost, like with Nancy all over again. Only this time, older, I had discovered booze to make me bolder—and less frightened of rejection.

But she did not reject me, and it was a tender time, so

different with her than with other girls. With other girls I was
a bit of a bully, on the runs down the coast, but I did not care
about other girls, not really, and there were girls, Brighton or
Margate, I'd ditched, left late at night for acting prim.

I could do that sober, the drink worn off, yet meeting with
Katie I required some booze. I could not somehow meet her
sober, and if I was using the booze, a fluttering heart, it was
not right that I needed it.

Why?

The guts, the thrill to hold her hand, to kiss her? She
wanted kissed. That she was coloured? I had been with a
boy. Her brothers? I was wary but not scared of them—I
was to prove that I was not scared of them. No, I know it
now, it was that I had found my ruin, that with Nancy and
her brother, I had missed.

I was inching closer, insidiously to the pit, my years of
torture.

Insidiously?

It might be, meeting Katie, that I looked forward more,
with fondness, to the booze than her.

For my schoolgirl lover I have some words of praise. Why
not? She cost me dearly, but she truly was a beauty. The
sweep of her brow to long black lashes. I marvelled at the
pinks of her nails, the whites of her eyes, and how her belly,
a honey hue, was splashed with the thickest, most inky bush.

She was wonderfully built in a wonderful way. Feminine.
Submissive. The smell of her, a hint of jasmine, and I would
I think have hung in there, have married her, if it wasn't for
her family, her brothers, their attention.

There had already been some muted threats at my interest
in their sister. I shrugged them off, like if they scowled or
bad-eyed me I'd smile at them. I thought the brothers full of
shit, though I don't know why and was alone in my thought.

I still went with the pack at weekends, the runs down the
coast and Katie not there—the brothers' strict hand—a new
girl on my pillion.

It was hard to refuse an empty saddle: girls all around and wanting to go.

This did not please the brothers.

It didn't please me that they shut away their sister.

A night in the pub with a few of my mates, the help of the booze, I told a brother (the youngest one) to take a fuck.

He was knife-thin but lithe with a wiry toughness, all gristle and muscle, like he was eighteen or nineteen years old. There is a big difference between that and sixteen and skinny, shot out of balance.

Looking back now at the boy that was me, I must have been daft, the best meaning of the word, that or more lover, in love, than I thought to be.

This brother had the sharpest head—tight fit of curls to a definite point. I thought him a freak, his head, and could only marvel he was Katie's brother.

I remember a belly laugh in the pub at his head, but too, when he was gone, the first open confrontation, I thought it best I had a weapon. Next day I bought a knife, a four-inch blade, that I carried down my stocking front.

It was not, and this I could not understand, as if Katie had been a virgin.

I could embellish upon that time, that summer, but it's best I think if I cut it short—September when the brothers hit me.

I had been drinking, a night in the pub and they knew where I drank and how I drank, and it was dark then at nights when, alone, the gang had burst up, some gone with girls, I staggered home.

The first thing I knew a hammer brushed my ear to crash my shoulder, the fleshy part of the curve of my neck. The pain was sickening. We were in a narrow side street, almost an alley. I went for the knife. The hammer bounced off my head and I heard them yell to kill me. It was the first I knew it was the brothers. The whole clan of them and all with hammers. It certainly seemed the whole clan of them with hammers, or clubs from the whacks I took and had I fallen I would, I'm sure, those bastards meaning business, have been crippled, confined to a wheelchair. At the very least I would have been crippled. As it was, though badly hurt, blinded with blood—for a time I thought to have lost an eye—I had out my knife and was slashing wildly.

The fight burst then. I have a dim recall of screaming sirens, and somehow, though I don't know how, I will never know how, I made it home to Anton's door.

I was burst inside, spitting blood—great gurds of it, and I was wracked with pain from my broken bones. I blacked out to waken two days later in a hospital bed.

I awoke like a mummy, so bandaged and plastered that I could but wriggle my fingers and toes. The doctors told me I was lucky, that I would live, but, it was touch and go whether I lose or I keep my left eye.

I prayed in that hospital, the first I had prayed since Glasgow, in the chapel at the head of the street, prayed that they would save my eye, no bit of plastic in my head.

The cops came and I told them I didn't remember.

They didn't believe me.

But I would say no more and they left me alone to pray for my eye.

It was a mean week in that hospital, the fate of my eye, waiting and thinking that Katie might visit but just some of the guys and Anton came. Anton came every visiting time, with fruit and flowers and I grew fond of the hunchback. He was a decent man. One of the few decent men I had met in London.

I was in hospital all of a month and not too bad the last three weeks when, just healing, knowing they had saved my eye, I had time to think about getting out of London, away from the brothers, who, or so I heard, were still for killing me.

I had lost my love, if that it was, for Katie. First I hated her for her lack of concern, but as time passed, one week to two, I simply forgot her.

I wished to forget the whole affair, so when the guys visited me I sold my scooter and what things I had, determined to go home, to depart from London while still whole. The place had proved a bit too much, both fun and terror with a nightmare end and I thought my next walk would be direct to Euston Station.

It rained, a silver fall from a heavy sky, hint of fog, the day I went—the weather and the leaden sky recalled the day of my coming, a kid looking for a tent in Piccadilly Circus.

Going out into the air, the crowded streets and motor traffic after a month of quiet, hushed wards, I felt strange and weak and not a little shaky. I thought about a drink to steady me. Whisky. So I stopped for a couple. I was now more gaunt, taller, a sickly pallor, and found no trouble getting served. Whisky. I thought beer too much, too long the effect that I desired.

A couple became a few. The pub a dump, wino haunt, outside of the station. But good whisky. I soon felt the whisky warm my gut and worm in my head. A delightful feeling, sense of well-being and I was not going home with nothing. No. I had a fist of notes on a time when a pound could get you drunk.

I dallied in that pub to arrive not in Glasgow but Manchester. It was night and raining and out of my roll I had one five pound note left, that and a thirst. I now wanted beer. A gallon at least. But if I hit the beer it hit me back and I ended in the model. Penniless. You slept with your shoes, only I didn't know on the first night, and next day I was barefoot. It was the lowest I'd been, barefoot in the model, and first begging the modeller's something to eat.

The next night, a bit more wise, when the lights went out I stole a pair of boots. It was that kind of place, like that you could always catch a rookie. In the model in Manchester where, then, the swing of the times; poverty beaten, there was no need to have a model. No booze, there was no need

to have a model. But it was there and so was I and it was a
guy in the model got me a job.

I went to work for the city cleansing. It paid well, though
you worked long hours, Saturday and Sunday and every
night late. You got used to the rats—true corkers—I
watched them mate, they did it like humans, no back-tail
stuff for those big brown rats—and general filth.

My pal, a brute of a man, bog Irish, and I worked a
tin-can press. The job was hard, heavy and foul raking the
cans—they fell down from above, from conveyor belts,
from out of wire cages. Sometimes rats leapt inside the
cages and got trapped in the jangle of cans, you never saw
so many cans, and we raked out the rats and pressed them
too.

The job was piece work, you got paid an amount for the
weight of the cans you pressed and you can press a hell of a
lot of cans to a cube, a weighed block of say twenty, thirty
pounds.

They supplied you with protective clothing, overalls and
high thick gloves, clog-like boots and such joy was the end
of each shift, a shower and change and pots of ale.

My pal, model mate, Fingal, was a bottle of wine a
morning man. He would scoff the stuff like ginger beer. I
had never seen anything like it, a couple of tips to empty the
bottle.

I of course admired the brute, for brute he was with an
animal strength, amazing endurance, the way he drank and
how he worked for, for all the cubes we pressed and loaded
to a trolley, he shifted four to every one of mine.

Yet we got paid the same, it was an even split if uneven
load, and I felt a cheat enough to treat Fingal to a bottle of
wine. In the mornings. Sometimes. Ten o'clock. I would
have bought the stuff the night before, a big green bottle,
the cheapest plonk, but what he liked. So some mornings,
most mornings, for it got that he expected it, he drank two
bottles of wine.

He would have been in his early fifties. This man loved wine—though he drank beer too and would not say no to whisky—worked as a beast and lived in the model. Yet, surprise, he could quote from Marx to Thomas Mann and Jack London—names which meant nothing to me then. We spent nights in the Manchester pubs until after the last bell, I would help carry him home to our model.

The days went on, he drank his wine and sent, as I did, some money home for a mother and wife and, his words, 'pack of brats' in County Clare, where in his youth, before the drinking, he must have demolished the local library, from *White Fang* to *Buddenbrooks*, the *Wars of the Roses*, the novels of Dickens and Hitler's *Mein Kampf*. I learned a bit, I learned to read from the Irishman, who was done with reading and living, his love now for wine, strong waters.

I moved after a couple of pay packets to a room away from the model, that flea-pit hole, where I had seen again what drink can do.

I saw death, men choke in their vomit, sleep not to awake, and that, the place, the keepers, the police, the morgue of the city, was not at all unusual. Just another stiff, and not all of them old, some guys in their twenties carted to the pauper's lot, the limestone pit.

I swore after that place, the sights I saw, wolf-like men, guys of thirty looking sixty, to never drink wine. I blamed the wine—I could hardly blame whisky when there was no whisky or whisky drinkers there.

In this period, I drank very little. I was intent on saving and hearing Fingal with his talk of books and authors, I would have preferred a visit to the library to a session in a pub. And now that Christmas was approaching, I wanted to go home.

My departure was hastened by the croaking of Fingal, who, for a time, on cold black mornings had complained of a pain in his chest or a pain in his side and one morning fell down dead. He died—I can but compare it, the place, the rats, the tatters he wore—as a slaughterhouse beast. One moment alive, working, raking out the cans, the rats, the next—and before he hit the deck—he was dead.

Morning.

Ten past nine, just one bottle of wine.

I had liked the man, he was a hard guy not to like, and I thought it meant he had drunk just one bottle of wine when another was in my pocket.

I quit that same day and I was on the Glasgow train before noon.

There was a Christmas tree inside the station; and Buchanan Street, the length of Argyle Street, all the way to Glasgow Cross, was strewn with fairy lights. Christmas, 1960. My hair was short and my trousers tight, cuffed around the ankles. Floyd Patterson was heavyweight champion. Tram cars still ran. Clanked. Big one-eyed yellow insects. It's what they looked like and I felt that I had never been away from this city.

I returned with a bag, some gifts and yet my mother, my sister, some weird taboo, we could not touch, hug or hold to show a physical affection. I gave out my gifts feeling a stranger. Why this lore of the slum, poor Glasgow life? I loved them dearly and they loved me, but returning, some inches taller, the core of me a different person, we could not burst that old taboo.

The London cockneys they'd kiss and cry and at the end of it all hold a party.

I knew.

The house was the same—my mother and sister, the cats on the stairs, the domed roof of the chapel at the head of the street.

We ate. The table was big and square and it filled the room, squeezed the kitchen. I sat with a view to the window, the winter nights. There were lighted trees in the tenement windows. I remember the trees, there were some that blinked, flicked out and in, on and off, and I learned that my child was dead. Aborted.

The pain of this news, so unexpected, fucked up my return, my homecoming.

I got drunk that night. A queer, sad sorrow. In a pub over the river where no one knew me.

The pub was an old-time joint with a sawdust floor, and a coal fire, and bragging a touch of colour, festive light—I remember the gantry, a bell and a star, some streamer ribbon, and red on white with big block letters MERRY XMAS. But not for me. I had never felt so miserable. The barman was fat, pot-bellied, with meaty arms and hands. I drank, he served. His assistant, a haggard blonde, the motherly sort, asked me what was wrong—where did I come from and where were my pals? I told her to fuck off, to leave me alone. The fat barman and a few of his customers threatened to kick me out. But the thing passed over and so did the night.

I awoke anyway in my own bed with nothing more than a headache. This was to be my last hangover, sore head, for almost three years.

I went off the stuff, I don't know why, there was no conscious effort—those, the conscious efforts, times, pledges, when I gasped for a drink—were to come much later.

I quit drinking at a time, an age when most boys, kids feeling their oats, were just beginning. And I did not, not for a moment, miss the booze or feel as if I missed it, for lacking in practice I was not, whatever else, a born alcoholic, as later in AA meetings I heard some members profess to be.

During the sober three years I furthered my reading. The library was in McNeil Street, just up from the Pig and Whistle. You could, on a visit to the library, almost smell the beer in the Pig and Whistle.

My reading was an orgy, it is the only word, no passing fad, going on for months, book after book, and the wonder was that my eyesight held. And yet for all the reading I still could not spell or punctuate the letters I wrote—for applications for jobs, I had hoped (we could afford it now) to become a motor mechanic. It took a long time for me to learn to spell, to hold grammar.

I did not get apprenticed as a motor mechanic, I was a little too old, almost seventeen, though I tramped the streets and visited a hundred garages, at least a hundred garages, almost begging a start. I tried then for a job as a fireman, but for a fireman I was too young, so at my age, stuck between, I went back to labouring. I worked in a whole bunch of jobs, dead-end shots, a boy labourer.

During this time, I would sometimes, with a girl, spend time in lounges, but I myself remained teetotal.

In Glasgow. Where I saw, I would have required blinkers not to have seen, my old flame, Nancy. I saw her first, a surprise, a week or so after I came home, in the shoe shop where she worked. I had no idea. The shop was not local. She wore a cotton smock. Blue. Knee-length. It went with her eyes. We did not speak. An icy silence. Strangers. And afterwards, on the street, passing, it was the same. There was nothing there, not even a dislike and not long after that I heard that she was married.

Her brother was still pally, but he was changed—dear Christ how changed—lanky now and with a foxy look so that what appeal he had was gone forever. I was embarrassed in his company, so avoided him and he got the message.

I was getting the message. I had seen too much of hardship. I determined to improve my lot, make money. I wanted a car, good clothes, tickets for the London fights. But that kind of money you would never get, not working for someone else. It took me all of a day to reason that. So I quit my job to open a second-hand shop. I bought and sold anything and everything, and soon, in a remarkably short time, I had four second-hand shops and all of them made money. They made a lot of money, not always from honest dealing. I doubt whether there are any second-hand shops that you can call honest, you work too close a fence, with stolen stuff, you want to make quick money. And the same with scrap-metal—I bought a half-share in a scrap-metal yard and it made more money than the four shops put together.

At nineteen years old I had my car, one of that year, good clothes, the money for travel, for the London fights, and if I gloss over this, success of a sort, it is because I think it fitting. I did not drink. I made money. There was nothing in my later drinking, near hobo state, I can blame on that time.

From sixteen to nineteen I had no cause or wish to drink. Life was good, no complications. I read still, still stayed at home, but disaster in the sweetest guise, the shape of a boy, was lurking round the corner.

This was to be the worst. I could have taken anything other than that, my love for a boy, for love it was and sprung on me who did not want it—by God I didn't—in the instant of a blink.

In a snooker hall, a working man's club—I was with a couple of pals—just passing an afternoon.

You entered the place up wooden stairs. A balcony looked onto a games room below. It was grubby and shabby, a dirty floor, guys playing cards and indoor bowls. I leaned against the balcony. Smoking. I remember smoking, the click of the balls, the waft of the smoke, how I was dressed, as when a child I remembered the carnival through the trees over the river. The clearest recall, as if time stuck in the instant that he entered. A boy who stirred me as no other boy, or girl at that had ever stirred me, and a feeling I would never know again.

I could not from the start shift my eyes from him. I was astonished and embarrassed that I could not shift my eyes from him. He was dark with combed-down hair, a Beatle cut and still at school with a school-bag and blazer: he wore grey flannel trousers.

I watched him play, stretch out: his head, arse and thighs, under the bright lights. I lingered there to watch him play and felt a choke in my throat, sweat on my brow. But a bastard place, the crudest talk, to admire and sneak glances at a boy, a total stranger.

Added to that, I was shaken myself that I should sneak glances at a boy, a total stranger.

My pals and I went out to a pub where, the first for almost three years, I had a drink. It was a surprise to them and a surprise to me that I had a drink. Whisky and beer. We all three treated a round. And if shaken, downcast till then, I left that pub a new man—high-spirited, surging with power, not giving a damn.

I went back to the snooker hall with expectations, hoping to look and admire, but the boy had gone.

I think I returned to the pub. It would have been my way, after a taste of booze, wanting more, even after three years I would have wanted more. Of that I am certain. But the night is clouded, and where I went—a night in the pub, out with a girl, just a walk around—I do not know.

Next morning the boy was in my head. I smoked in bed and thought about him. All of the day, grey winter November, he was in my head. I had a few drinks at lunchtime, pints of beer and thought about him. And I wondered what the fuck was wrong with me that a boy, a stranger, a moment, could have such effect? I sat alone drinking as, in the future, I was to sit alone with many a drink and not always drinking beer. No. I had money enough for faster effect, and right from the start, from the night before, at intervals for long years after, I drank this time for sheer effect.

That night at four o'clock, I was again in the snooker hall. Standing. Leaning against the banister. And if not drunk I was not sober. Smoking. A white coat on. I knew some, most of the guys, mostly small-time thugs and thiefs who loitered there and we all of us smoked, and the place, like the London joint—the gangster's parlour, was like peering through a fog.

I stood. Impatient. Big. I was if lithe much heavier now, a solid weight and if still boxing I would have fought as middle. But my mind that night was far from boxing. Waiting. I felt a freak waiting. A schoolboy with his schoolbag—what if the guys around knew my head, the purpose of my visit? It was my constant dread as time passed by, that they might twig, for it was not my scene, that place, not really, and neither was the way I felt.

I was about to go, depart, for it was long past four, when he walked in. My heart leapt. Literally. The very sight of him. I leaned back against the balcony. He wore still the blazer and his schoolbag, but had switched his pants to a light tight denim.

He seemed well-known in the place, and nothing shy, rather the opposite, rather pushy—I fancied that he was pushy, a kid with spunk and I liked the thought that he was pushy, a kid with spunk. Modern. His Beatle haircut, pointed shoes, tight denims—the other stuff, school blazer and bag, just made him different as a touch of class, innocence: if, as I later learned, he was far from innocent. Again, I watched him play. A closer view. He wore a blood-red jersey. His chest looked strong, but his shoulders were slender, fragile almost, and—he strained the denim with his arse and thighs—a wonderful perfection to me who felt like a monster for the observation. Study. His head, hair, the line of his brow, flare of his nose. He had the biggest impact, and I can see him still. How he was. His smile and how his hands, slender fingers, had dirty nails.

He would leave about six-thirty or seven, and I left with him—out for my evening drink.

There was a particular pub, it was just over the way,

outside of the snooker hall, where—it had a quiet lounge and heartbreak music—I had chosen for my drinking.

And I drank. There was now nothing to stop me, for I had plenty of money and was legally old enough to sit in that place, indulge my habit, wonder at the boy, think the fondest thoughts. Invariably leaving I was drunk, not falling-down drunk—but drunk enough to drive too fast, to not have driven at all.

But even with no car I was drinking too much, and drinking alone, a sure depressant—I felt the depression in the mornings. But I blamed the boy and not the whisky. How could I blame the whisky when a couple more drinks and the depression lifted? Indeed, for this was a difficult time, I thought the whisky and the surcease it gave, was all that kept me going.

I went back to the snooker hall night after night. Four o'clock. Six-thirty or seven, the kid gone home, I would be in the pub. I would stay for the music, such sad songs, for a couple of hours. Usually. Though once I recall I stayed till shutting. I was rolling drunk that night and the barman begged my car keys. I was by then something of a regular, a good customer because of the money I spent. It made a good excuse for a return next morning.

So from the start, after not a week back drinking I was also drinking mornings. I should explain that in some Glasgow pubs, after nights of drinking in the way I drank, you are thought a regular very soon.

In a few pubs I was soon thought that, a regular. Inside of a week I was up to drinking, in bar measures—I still at this time did not drink at home—a bottle a day and some days more. That not counting the beer and I drank a lot of beer. Especially in the morning I drank a lot of beer. That was the first week. The second week I was drinking more, an all-day thing, morning till night, but drinking the best—a five-star malt—it did not hit me as it should. It took years to hit me as it should.

There was even in the first week's drinking some pride in

the liquor I could hold. I thought about other guys, what booze it took to make them fall, and that I was tougher, stronger. In any case I suffered little, just as I said from the morning blues and I thought I knew the cause of them.

Looking back, but for that boy I would not have drunk, not then, and might never have drunk.

As it was, my frightful lust—for no other boy or male would trouble me again—I didn't know what way to turn and the bottle was my only solace.

After a week or two of nightly visits at four o'clock I was playing the kid at snooker. His name was Tony. He was easy and free with a nice nature, and my game was to anchor the cue ball so as to have him stretch, lean out over the table under the lights. But it was not enough, and, soon, I was waiting outside to run him home.

He stayed in a tenement better than mine, red sandstone facing near Shawfield, a football stadium, and *he* asked *me* to take him out.

Daytime.

I asked about school.

'I'll dodge it.'

In my car, windows up, outside his close and I could almost feel the heat of him.

'I've dodged it before,' he told me.

'You hiv?'

'Aye.' He smiled. Conspiratorial. 'You,' he said, 'kin write me a note, say I was sick.'

I smoked.

He smoked.

I liked it that he smoked, Christ, I liked it that his nails were dirty and I would write many a sick-note in days to come.

'It's best,' he said, 'daytime.'

'It is?'

'Aye.' Again the smile, and quite a game this flirt with me. 'Besides,' he said, 'I don't like school.'

'I hated it.'

'You did?'

'Aye.'

'How old are you?' Blue-grey eyes, a quizzical look.

'Nineteen.'

'I'm fourteen.' And a sure fourteen. How he sat, looked at me, who did not run him home for nothing, gave him money, if only a little, without a motive and he knew that.

My problem in those long days and drunken nights was I did not know my motive. Or I was scared to admit it, even to myself. And I did like Tony, as a person, and the more that I knew him the better I liked him. Yet at the root of it all for that boy and me, and from the first, from the moment I saw him, it was a physical thing. But such a fumble, as if he were a china doll.

There was in the mind of the youth I was, a sense of ridicule in the love of a boy. How I felt just did not suit me and once again, with another lover, a deeper love, I wished that we had never met.

It was a crazy time, not him but me and my stupid act. Drinking. It got that (shades of Katie, but a lot more booze) I could not meet him sober. If I met him at noon-time I'd had a few and in my car I had a bottle. But even with the booze it was still awkward, the most awkward time (which should have been the best time) of all my life.

The thing dragged on, my drinking increased. I bought him a watch for a Christmas present. He almost hugged me for the gift and I could, I know, have held him then—at least I could have held him. But I was still so reluctant, scared that a night, a watch, might ruin it all. What? I still don't know. For sex was the root—without sex, physical attraction, there was nothing between that kid and me.

He knew, I knew: so why the fuck my fatherly act?

But it could not last. I think we both knew that it could not last. That there was nothing fatherly in my affections.

I took him sometimes, matinées, to the movies. We saw

El Cid. January. I would turn twenty in February. If not in the nuthouse—from my nights in the pub, the sad, sad songs—I would turn twenty in February.

Tony, I saw all the time—if not in the flesh then in my head—his smile, his voice so I could concentrate on nothing. It was impossible to work. And I was drinking money and losing money and it was downhill all the way.

I, with my innocent act, a show as stupid as my drinking, mooned about like some love-sick (and I was sick all right, even Tony enquired about my drinking) moron good for violence. The bubble burst. I could take no more, sick in the soul and sick in the head, the night that Ali (then Clay) fought Sonny Liston.

I asked Tony who he thought would win.

'Liston.'

'I think Clay.'

It was late, I was drunk. It was one of the few late nights we had together. In my car, outside the snooker hall, where at ten o'clock or closer to eleven I had picked him up. It was late anyway to buy a morning newspaper. Clay and Liston were on the front page. Liston looked a bear but I thought to see something in Clay. Tony saw something in me, the booze I had shifted—an all-day session—and not the man or youth he knew. No. I was drunk all right and tougher, more rough with him and I could be very rough, much tougher than he knew. I had not my car and the trimmings for nothing. He said not a word, no protests, I drove him to a place I knew, where before, with girls, I had been.

When it was over I felt so lousy I can't explain.

'You still think Liston?'

The night was dark.

Tony said nothing.

You could hear the wind, the gusts outside.

I drank some whisky from the bottle I kept.

Outside the night, the wind and rain.

Tony sat smoking. In the half-light. Tears glistened on his

cheeks. I loved him more than ever. Then. In my car. And there nothing dirty or perverted about it, just how in my roughness I'd bruised his pride and hurting him had hurt myself.

I was still half drunk and getting drunker. It was one of the times I was scared to get sober.

I was just nineteen, too young for this and the pain I felt for that boy that night, feeling so roguish, dirty, near suicidal.

'You feel okay?'

'It's late,' he said.

'I'll get you home.'

Driving. I should not have been driving. Swigging at whisky. And how I felt, like that, that boy and me, a head-on smash might solve it all.

Playing music. Smoking. I drove with no lights. Tony pointed it out. I switched them on. He told me that I drove too fast.

'You want to get home.'

'I want tae get home alive.'

I slowed a bit.

'It's okay,' Tony said. 'I mean, you know—'

'Sure.'

'You're—'

'What?'

'I don't know.'

'I know how you mean.'

'You do?'

'I think so.'

'Nobody'll know.'

'No.' I wanted to hold and to comfort him, but it was no good with the way I felt. I knew what he meant, how I'd caught him, ragged underwear, and his stupid shame just added more weight to the load that I carried. 'Not if you don't tell them they won't!'

I dropped him off outside his close.

Late.

It must have been two, three o'clock, easily two or three o'clock, for I remember I asked him what he would say—where he had been.

I got drunk next day, or still drinking that morning, I did not sober up. Clay beat Liston and I had a bet, one hundred pounds at seven to one that Clay would beat Liston. It was two weeks or more before I collected. I got so drunk. But again, and again I must stress, not falling-down drunk. I just lost interest. It was my first true bender. In a hotel. I just booked in and spoke to no one.

But my head nagged me. The sober moments were early mornings. For I knew it was all wrong. Holed-up drinking, guzzling whisky and I had jilted Tony, a date we had. It was a mean time. The hotel was good, it cost me plenty, but a miserable time, never going out, just drinking in the bar and in my room. The recall is fogged, but the fear that I was queer was very real indeed.

At the end of a week, eight days, no fun in the drunk—few of my drunks were ever fun—I sobered up enough to go home. I had no sweats, shakes, no sickness, nothing—just a dead feeling at the end of the bout. For a day or two I could not eat. Small penance for my orgy of drink: no reason to quit, though for a time I did slow down, cut back on the morning drinking.

The Gorbals now was a heap of rubble, that and brand new houses, tower blocks, and where I stayed—my mother, her tenement, was last to move—was truly grim.

Yet it seemed impossible to get her out.

Eight months, a year, we had lived alone in the tenement. A spooky place. All the other house doors open, like living in a ghost town. The water got cut off and we had to carry our own, and still—without toilets—my mother would not move.

I was worried, with reason, for one light in a tenement and winos squatting, moving in, guys needy or greedy, crazy, might kill you for a sixpence.

So nights I stayed with my mother. Who would not go. Move out. The most stubborn stand. She held up the work, tumble of a hundred years, the demolition of the tenement. I thought it funny and sad, councillors visiting, the housing threatening. I forget how much (a figure was quoted) she cost them a day. But it went on. I got used to it, the last stand in the tenement. Though, nights in a high wind, the whole place swayed and I got drunk sometimes and listened to music, the Beatles and Stones, something new in that old house two windows high.

It was no councillor's pleas—the threatening housing, and they did threaten, finally got my mother out.

My sister, she had a boyfriend of the snooty sort who was ashamed, mortified at the place she stayed in. So we moved, or they moved, a shift, not far—two miles at most— to a house with a loo, a bath, hot water and safety. No winds there or winds that threatened. I went to a flat, a place of my own. It was the end of an era, where, the place that long was home, was now empty sky.

I was by this time, March, drinking steadily, heavily, and there is no doubt that booze was the motivating factor in what happened next. I sold out on the shops, my share of the scrap-metal, I sold the lot to my partner, a hard-faced crook, for a crazy price to do a more crazy thing. I ran away. I was such a fool and a coward. The finest feeling I ever knew. And what the fuck did it *really* matter that it was a boy and not a girl?

I pause. Query my motives, how then I felt or thought to feel, for not only booze but age creeps in.

Certainly if there had been no booze I would not have sold out, not all that I had and not at the price. At a time when I did not need the money.

But as all caught up with a need to escape for I was not happy. There was some sense of unease. All the other guys, they went with girls. I was stuck on Tony and if I did not flaunt him, I did not hide him either.

But the whole thing and I was only twenty—and, I liked to think, a man's man—still puzzles me.

I will say no more of Tony. If I ran from him or ran from myself, but drop him now as I dropped him then. Sudden. He came and went if, a long time, even now, he lingers on, a good and healthy memory.

Early April, early morning, the sun high, a blue sky, the birds chirping—I took the birds for a good luck omen—I set out on my journey.

Journey?

I had no idea where I was headed. A morning in April, 1964. Just a need to move, new places. People. Cities. I felt as if I had been cooped-up too long, with a terrible energy. I burst with energy. Perhaps the booze, perhaps my age or a combination of both, but I could, that trip, whatever else, have done without the booze.

Lunchtime I was drinking south of Carlisle. I thought it nothing to get drunk and drive. I think I was pretty competent, a bit too fast but pretty competent at drunk-driving. I never, anyway, in all of my drinking, got caught drunk-driving or smashed a car. The pubs shut I continued south, toward London with a couple of kids, hitch hikers, for company.

The scene, the sixties, was swinging now. Children, a whole army, like a new crusade, and it might be that I should have gone to San Francisco.

The kids, we all smoked dope and headed for London—I felt free, as rid of chains, on the run to London, where in the morning, I had no intention of going.

Any place but London.

Still we headed there, the kids—a boy and girl, teenagers—and me.

We played music, I treated them to dinner and it was late at night when I dropped them off in Soho.

I stayed just three, four days in London, but long enough for my car to be stolen. I reported the theft and found out Anton was dead—I paused to enquire—then moved on. I moved by train and boat to Jersey. I shifted my drink from whisky to brandy in a duty-free bar on the boat to Jersey. I would shift, see-saw from whisky to brandy before, more or less, I settled for wine. They all had much the same effect, and wine drinking, before the meth-drinking, I thought to be mad the whisky-drinking, the money I had spent. I got drunk of course on the brandy, the boat to Jersey. A trip of five or six hours, it poured with rain. Parked at the bar, the rain didn't bother me, the brandy was good and I puffed a cigar. It seemed, a cigar, the brandy, the proper thing. On the boat to Jersey I met a woman who was as rich as she was handsome and she was very handsome. Statuesque. She asked my name and told me hers, Jaqueline, and I had never known a woman so forceful, forward, drinking like a man.

But she could hold the booze, no stupid talk and we got along, with a meal together and a battle of sorts as to who would pay.

But I got the price of that meal a hundred times over.

In Jersey.

There was a car to meet her.

She took me home.

Her house was hotel-big and white and built on a cliff facing out over the sea. She stayed with her brother, who too had a taste for brandy. The brother was older, a good twenty years by the look of him, long snow-white hair and a goatee beard. He welcomed me as a long-lost friend. Drunk. He was drunk and I was drunk and Jaqueline was running close.

The brandy flowed, this was about eight at night, and the brother, a doctor, a gentle man, you could tell by his face that he was a gentle man, professed to be a judo black-belt or an expert at karate. Something like that and some Germans (the war, the occupation of Jersey) dead at his deadly hands.

I flung in with a lie or two, I forget what rot, but something daft to equal him.

But enough said about that man on that night, a good man, sensitive, not the heart to kick a cat, we got roaring drunk and in the morning he did not know me.

I awoke in the morning with the sun in my eyes, a view over the sea; the sky much lighter than the sea and Jaqueline curled beside me.

It was the grandest room. High. A polished wood floor, four-poster bed, scattered rugs and the view, from huge windows, was really something.

Breakfast.

The brother had a bad dose of the shakes. He looked at me with bleary eyes and I knew he did not know me.

Jaqueline, Jacky—I called her Jacky—was steady as a rock, showered and fresh. That woman could drink, but again, I got to know her and she was no drunk—the difference is mighty between a drunk and a drinker. The brother shook, I swear, so that his goatee wagged and needing a drink, brandy in his coffee. Jacky, you would not have known she had been drinking, held off till night and then only took a couple.

It took more than a couple to steady Sebastian, the brother, who smoked and shook and laced his coffee, more brandy than coffee, and the man was a doctor.

I thought it funny, the guy, his shakes, brandy in the morning, a doctor.

Then I thought it funny.

I shook myself, and I would shake as bad, worse than him—in much grimmer surroundings I was to shake as bad, worse than him—it was far from funny.

I can think of nothing less funny.

In a palace or cave booze is a great leveller—I think only

love, the truest sort, is such a leveller—there is nothing funny in the shakes.

They were a black-eyed pair, my hosts, long-faced, French—the surname was French and Sebastian was free with the brandy.

'I forget your name.'

I told him.

'Of course,' he said, but without a clue.

Jacky, my first older woman, statuesque, nothing sagging, was good for me, a good companion and good in bed. The affair was free and easy. No future. We both knew there was no future, that I would move on, or, if I delayed too long she would weary of me. I suffered no illusion that the house was a permanent home. And I did not want it to be a permanent home. I wanted to move. Such wanderlust. But I was content for a time, not long but a time, and I made a friend in Sebastian.

Man who shook, who hardly ate. I did not in all the time I was there, about a month, see Sebastian eat a decent meal.

I had a hearty appetite, if only for my age—I could eat and drink the whole day long—and I worried that man, that he hardly ate.

Yet he had a wonderful manner even when drunk, telling lies, killing Germans, as you got to know him you got to like him—and I liked Jacky too, respected her who, with no pretence, was just using me as I used her.

A good arrangement.

There was nothing wrong in the whole set-up, the month I spent in Jersey.

I have a fondness for Jersey for that time. Sebastian, the drunkard he was—about twice a year he went to hospital, to a drying-out ward in England—who first warned me of my own drinking, the curse that booze can soon become.

It was, this warning, the only time that I did not like Sebastian.

I who did not shake, who ate.

'Just a tip,' he said, a wink, 'old boy.'

But I was not old, I was young and strong, headstrong, and who the fuck did he think he was?

I was quite annoyed that the doctor, the first of many a doctor, should speak that way, 'Just a tip, old boy,' about my drinking.

And yet, that man, I know it now, he was concerned. The hell of his days, shakes in the morning; a sickness—and it is a sickness—that he could not cure. But where he had been I had yet to go. And this was not a trip I'd want again. But I would not be warned off. And his tip, the best one—it was worth a hundred winning horses—I took for a fucking insult.

Then.

In Jersey.

Where, to the island's pubs, some of them quaint as other centuries, delightful places, I was a frequent visitor.

But I cycled too, on an ancient bike, big and upright, and swam the bays and coves. I was in good shape, filling out, a flat chest, muscled belly, when I left for France and train to Paris.

I just took the notion one day, a trip to France, the lights of Paris.

There were no sad farewells when I decided to go, but a drink with Sebastian as he welcomed me back. Any time. His Jersey home. Sweet Interlude. Jacky. No tender lover but she suited me then. As though with her I'd proved myself. It was how I thought.

Sebastian ran me to the quay, the boat—I had come on a whim and was departing on a whim. It was how I moved at that time, on the roads, the cities of Europe, a generation moved. A time of wastage, bittersweet, but it had to be, the boy was me and it had to be.

I was drunk as I set my first foot in France. St Malo. The sun beat down and at an outside cafe, I proceeded to get drunker. I don't know why for I was elated enough on my first journey abroad, but I got drunk enough to miss the Paris train.

I stayed the night in a room in the cafe where I drank. It was old-fashioned, a clean room, decent bed, but in the morning there was an outrageous charge. I was swindled on my first night in France. But I did not protest (I was still not sure about the money, francs to pounds) and paid the bill and continued on to Paris.

Paris. I stayed in an hotel close to the Gare du Nord. Sober. I checked in sober. I had no intention of getting robbed and was mad at myself, the night before, for paying the bill. The day wore on, no booze, my head clearing, the madder I got. I worked myself up to a fury, to consider to go back. But stuck in the train—and it was as well that I stuck in the train—I would have gone to jail on a return to St Malo.

But as I got to Paris, and maybe it was not bad, in retrospect maybe it was not bad, for I got to Paris sober.

A fine temper, but sober, brusque and sharp—I could now divvy the money, francs to pounds as swift as a teller—I demanded to inspect my room, what value I would get for my money.

The wrong attitude, mood, for a visit to Paris, but I got over it. My first night out I got over it. I was fascinated with Paris. For all of a week I hardly slept. I drank, but wasn't drunk. I was never drunk in Paris. I drank in a way that if I had continued to drink I would still be drinking. Something about the place. Then. I have been back to Paris and drunk, drinking a way no man should drink, so no magic in a city was magic to me a long, long time ago.

I dallied in Paris for more than a month, until, for no reason, or reason I could fathom, it loomed as phoney as a wax museum.

Suddenly.

It might be a queer thing to awake one morning and think Paris a fraud. But I did. And so much a fraud that the very same day, I got a train for Spain. Irun. And on to Barcelona. It was the beginning of a love of Spain, its people, who incredibly—I thought it incredible—still reeled from the effects of the Civil War. Beggars abounded. The kids ran scruffy. Bare-foot. You saw from the train, the run from Irun to Barcelona, black-clad women work in the fields. And the further south you went the fiercer the poverty, hotter the sun, but I liked the place, the people who despite the poverty, or made manifest by the poverty, were a nobility in rags.

I stayed some days in Barcelona, first visit to a brothel— the girls lined up, you took your pick, as in restaurants, you wanted fish; there live ones swam and again a pick. The place was earthy and old, I thought older than Paris, more earthy, and you could climb a hill and see the sea, the city, villas and hovels, and the rich were rich and the poor were poor, and of course, with this split in society—strutting *guardia* all leather and guns—I sided with the poor.

The further inland, away from the coast and the tourists, the more beggarly poverty, smells, open sewers, old women working, near-naked children, crippled men, I sided with the poor.

And yet what was not right became the place, and I would rather Spain then, how it was, to how post-Franco it has become.

I got drunk in Spain. Fundador brandy. I drank it by the bottle and I liked the bars, *bodegas*, dark and wet, on the bar, seafood that you got for free. You could make a meal of that stuff, little fish, shrimps and shells, eat it by the handful. It saved on time, the trouble of a restaurant. So I thought then but thinking now my appetite had begun to wane. This was no one-week, eight-day stint, but constant drinking. Sustained. I was a long time, five months in Spain, and till the last, till in Madrid I almost croaked, the drinking was constant and sustained.

I crossed from Barcelona to Ibiza, Ibiza to Majorca, Majorca to Valencia—where they had made *El Cid*—and from Valencia inland to Madrid. There were other stops, other places. I did not travel direct from Valencia to Madrid. Some days, on a bus, I would travel only twenty miles. Other days a hundred miles, it matters little, as little by little I got to Madrid.

It was the hottest city, no question, in all of Spain the hottest city and the slums, true hovels, were the worst slums I had seen till then. I saw, in daylight, rats in the streets—could you call them streets—of Madrid, where, a wise man, you do not go in high summer.

I visited in August. The sun beat down with hammer force. Barcelona, Valencia, the Balearics, or even Seville—and it can be hot in Seville—they all seemed as cool as April or May. I should have got out of Madrid, away from the oven. The heat, humidity, was atrocious. Midday you just could not walk. And night or morning when you did, the heat still hung, as if seeped up from the ground. Man and beast were toasted, fried. Dogs yawned, cats slept, even the rats seemed lethargic. And yet the city functioned. Nobody running but still the city functioned.

I was not in the best of shape when I reached Madrid. My appetite, with the constant booze, had all but gone, and added to that, suddenly sprung, I had a grinding toothache.

It ended, the toothache, an upper molar, in a visit to the dentist.

Enrique Porfino. Dental surgeon. There were a few of us waiting for Enrique Porfino. A square room, cool, but any place under a roof was cool away from those streets. We grinned to one another and a wild-looking man clutching both his ears (I was, strange but true, to meet him again on a bus in Ireland, and still clutching his ears). He had the look of an angry bird. Enrique Porfino had all the sparkle of a geriatric. He was easily seventy, and as he tried for a pull, crunched my tooth so that I gave a scream. I was about two weeks in Madrid. He had then to slit the gum and scoop out the root. When it was done I thanked the guy. I was then taken into another room to rinse my mouth. There was some cramp in my gut and I asked for the loo. I had had cramps, real benders, along with the toothache, the past few days. I had dismissed them for wind or indigestion. But in the dentist's, another cramp, and I was hunched over as I made the closet.

First I thought it was a haemorrhage. Just a casual glance, a shudder, I thought it a haemorrhage. But the pain had gone and I felt better, more fit to walk after the loss of the blood.

I left the dentist to enter a bar, drink brandy. I had little or no knowledge of medicine, but I thought of an ulcer, bowel cancer, I thought of a lot of things, conditions, and I thought of a one-off, something coming and going, and I did feel better.

A few more brandies and I forgot the thing.

I had been always healthy, a strong constitution. I had prided myself, despite my drinking, upon my constitution. I could not see it let me down. I smoked and drank and thought about a visit to Malaga. I thought to get away from Madrid, the heat. So few, if any—I had met none—British people. The place, its slums, the Escorial—a gloomy monument, the Madrid equivalent of Versailles—depressed me. I would not forget that palace, as no other palace, as a tombstone, outside of Madrid.

I sat in the bar, thinking about getting out, away from this place where from the first, I had felt out of sorts—the city, its heat dreening me, sapping my strength.

Also, after this trip, seven months in a suitcase, the people I'd met and the places I'd stayed, my money was running out. I had enough I thought for a week in Malaga, but that was all—a week in Malaga and then it was home.

That was what I thought. Drinking the brandy. Fundador. I could drink two or three bottles a day. I had been drinking two or three bottles a day. I swirled the stuff inside my mouth, the gap of my missing tooth. Madrid. I hated the place. City. And what the fuck brought me here, to the capital of Spain? Where even the natives tottered in the heat. Where for other than the rich—a room in the Ritz or the Madrid equivalent—the hotels were old, bug-ridden—my room had a mouse—with shared facilities.

I made to go, to leave the bar for a *siesta*, when with all the force of a fist the cramps hit me again.

Sweat beaded my brow as I fumbled for the closet hunched over and with a hand to my gut.

The relief was like a shot of heroin, but the bucketing blood was frightening.

I went back to the bar for a couple more brandies, more worried now as this was no one-off and I would never make it, not how I felt, all the land-miles to Malaga.

I was half drunk and drinking and all I knew was when the cramps hit me I had to lose some blood to ease the pain.

Some blood.

I drank the brandy, like beer I drank it, and went back to my hotel, the room with the mouse. I had taken some comfort at the mouse, as after my experience with the Manchester cleansing, I knew that mice and rats don't go, mix together.

It was a nightmare walk from the bar to my hotel, not far, under the widest sky—it has that, Madrid, the widest sky in Europe—the beating sun.

I was lashed with sweat, it popped on the top of my head, seeped out of the pores of my belly.

The mouse was there, in my room—it was the boldest mouse and I sometimes fed it.

But not that day.

I slept a few hours to wake with the cramps, a visit to the closet. Not clean, a smell of shit, but if you travel in Spain, in the summer heat, you get used to that, the smell of shit.

My case, trouble, was not the shit but blood—and it could not go on, this losing blood.

I knew that it could not go on but hoped for it to stop.

Again, the blood, the cramps had gone. I puzzled at this. A haemorrhage would not just come and go like stop and start. Out of the closet sitting on the edge of my bed, smoking, drinking more brandy, wishing for beer but I was far too weak to even think of visiting a bar.

It was night. Black. I burned the light, a low-watt bulb. The mouse begged. I thought to see a doctor. I thought that next morning, if I was still the same I ought to see a doctor.

Again the brandy, and the insanity of booze. I sat on the bed swigging the stuff, it got me feeling better, indeed after some swigs from the bottle it got me feeling jolly.

I even fed the mouse some cheese—I bought the cheese especially.

If only the cramps would ease up, with no more blood after a couple of days I would be a new man, the old man. I had forgotten the toothache, the dentist, the pain of *that*, in my hope for the cramps to vanish.

I moved from the bed to the window. I felt light. Giddy. The booze in my blood. The room was as high as wide, a cube almost. A table and chair and worn carpet, ancient wardrobe. The windows opened in, not out, and beneath me, over the way, streetlights on, were a cobbled square and bar at the corner. I could not see the sky, the stars, the brightest, bluest stars, brilliant moon—I never tired at the wonder of the night sky of Madrid. But not tonight. I saw only the square, winking cobbles, the bar at the corner, and it was not unlike, on late summer nights, the old street in the Gorbals.

I had a couple more swigs. I had plenty of brandy, full bottles and retired to bed.

The mattress was lumpy but the bed was clean, no bugs. The last I remember on that day of despair, worry, pain, a too-old dentist, was the frolicking mouse—it entertained, or did its best, some cartwheels on the carpet.

I was again awakened, by now in the middle of the night, by the cramps in my gut. As if something were live, a beast down there. The pain hit me in spasms. I hobbled to the closet. The floor creaked. It was the loneliest night. I cursed Madrid. Sitting on the pan, blood and wind and wind and blood. My whole gut gurgled, and in that place there were bugs okay, they crawled on the ceiling and up the walls, I had to brush them from my legs.

You flushed the pan and it was like the whole place tumbling, falling down, a building older, a good century older than the oldest Glasgow tenement.

Again after the blood I had peace of a sort. Physical. But my gut still gurgled and I had no peace of mind. I feared for another attack. It was about three in the morning. I had awoken the mouse and would have kicked it had I the strength. Sitting again at the edge of the bed I drank some brandy. I was by then, I opened my eyes, conditioned to drink some brandy. It warmed me, my limbs, a first chill, shiver, in Madrid. That and my condition, it did more than that, just warm me, I was so fucked I couldn't care. And I needed the brandy, the first time in some months of drinking, I needed a drink. I know it now if I dismissed it then. And yet I was drinking little. Compared to what, on a night on the town, I would have drunk. But again, unfit, I should not have been drinking at all.

A couple more times that night I, weak now, having not the strength to fight the mouse, adjourned to the closet and for the first time that night I thought of death, my own, its manner and way and I hoped not now, not here.

I drank the brandy and thought to live, to see a doctor when the sun came up.

I slept a bit, dozed off and on, both hot and cold, my body drenched with sweat.

Sweat.

It dripped from my toes, my fingertips, the hair on my chest as if I were just out from a swim.

Morning.

The white hard light.

Familiar.

They served breakfast, black sweet coffee, from eight till ten—there were about six guests; a coal-black man who spoke to no one and a party of Dutchmen. The guy who ran the place was called just José—a long tall one, a gipsy look.

My room was one up, up stairs that creaked. The whole place creaked, the banister shook and it was as well that my room was just one up I was so weak that morning.

Drinking the black sweet coffee.

I asked José for the nearest doctor.

'You feel unwell, Miguel?!'

I laced the coffee with brandy, it was not the first morning I had laced my coffee with brandy and José rather than frown he thought me *mucho hombre*.

It was, I am sure, the Spanish male, the more you could drink the more *hombre* you were, why—as love at first sight—I had felt at home in the country.

In all of Spain except Madrid.

I rose to go, seek out the doctor, Don Lorenzo, when on the street, and it was muggy already that you could feel the build-up, the swing of the sun, the cramps hit me again and I knew it was no good, that I would never make it to the doctor.

Back in the closet, only now, this time, my gurgling gut, splashing blood, the pain did not go and in that animal place I was wracked by spasm after spasm.

I looked at myself, my face in the mirror (cracked) and it was the face of a stranger, wolf-like, caved-in cheeks, my teeth showed bigger and my nose more pointed, and I was all the more alarmed.

The spasms went, or subsided a bit and fit to walk, though sore to walk, I demanded the doctor. *Pronto.*

I went back to my room.

Waiting.

I swigged at the brandy.

The doctor came. He was brisk and sharp, I told him about my pain, the blood, he pressed my belly and a few more things, and pronounced that I had dysentery.

That was all?

I had known guys, children, a lot of them, who had dysentery in the old Gorbals.

The doctor spoke English well and the leading question was had I money—*dinero?*

I told him some, not much—dear Christ, had I much I would not have be staying here, in this hovel.

He asked—a whiff of my breath, the brandy on the table—did I drink heavily?

'I take a drink.'

'No more drink.'

'Just stop the blood. Get rid of the pain.' It was how I spoke. Sober, or not too drunk, it has how I spoke. Direct and to the point. 'I'll pay what you ask.'

'But no more drink,' he said.

'Sure.'

'You really should go to hospital.'

'I've no money to go to hospital.'

'Insurance?'

'No insurance.'

He sighed. 'You can send *home* for money?'

I shook my head—no—and I did not want to go to hospital.

'You should have insurance.'

'Look, you want to help me?'

'Of course.'

I waited.

He considered. 'You've lost a lot of blood.'

'You can stop it.'

'But no more drink,' he said, repeated.

'Just stop the blood, get rid of the pain.'

He rummaged in his bag, and I still don't know his treatment, what medicine—but some painful jags and a bottle of pills.

I paid him money, some pesetas, a lot of pesetas, and indeed I should have taken insurance for this treatment, whatever it was, it was not cheap.

He would, he said, return next day.

I was not too worried at dysentery, I'd never heard out of all the people I'd known, a single one to die from it.

But two problems. The brandy on the table, it took a manful effort to resist such a temptation, as apple in Eden, I did not succumb.

The cramps came and went. I staggered to the closet, took the pills and went back to bed. A bastard time, feeling so low, low in spirit, and the brandy, winking bottles of amber, like a still-life on the table.

I got through the day without a drink, too, but at night, all of a sudden, I took the shakes.

I was twice sick, from the booze I'd drunk and this sudden withdrawal.

And I don't know what was the worse, but I knew I had a mild dose of the horrors, the walls were closing in on me. And I attacked—no other word—the brandy.

I attacked it with no remorse, against the doctor's warning—I had drunk too much for too long for a sudden stop.

The shakes subsided. The walls and the room took on a proper perspective—but in the morning I was worse.

By God, I was. Blood pure and red, the biggest splash, and you could—one glance at the pan, my bright red blood—die from this.

You could easily die from this.

The doctor came.

I confessed my drinking and out went the brandy, four bottles or five.

I told him about my shakes, the walls closing in—I felt a

clown, but I had to get better, stop this thing—my life was flowing from me.

'A man like you should never drink,' he said. Then, and matter of fact, 'You'll die, you know, if you continue to drink.'

I had no cause, not how I felt, to doubt him—that I would die if I continued to drink.

But how he said it, as a black-wigged judge with no compassion, it didn't matter a fuck to him if I lived or if I died.

In Madrid.

He would do his best. I knew he would do his best, but if I lived or died, a grave in Madrid, it was all the same to him.

I got injected again, some stabs in the hips, and I got—vitamin B1—my first treatment for my drinking.

In effect after a small drama, if large to me, I recovered in that room. No more shakes, walls closing in, and the doctor came and went but we never got pally, I just paid him money and he got me better. Certainly, that man did not think me *mucho hombre*.

I had mixed feelings about him, because from the first, then each time he called, he seemed more concerned about the state of my wallet than my health.

It was the impression I got, and it cost me a lot—about all that I had—to get well.

By the time I was on my feet Malaga was out of the question.

I had money in Scotland, but little here and for the first time for years I felt the pinch—I would liked to have seen Malaga.

Instead I drank in the bar at the corner. The few days I stayed before I went I drank in that bar. With the locals. Guys who worked building or brushed the streets. They renewed my faith in the Spanish character. Sunday. *Domingo*. That was the day they all got drunk.

I held back for a bit, for a while I held back. After my sickness, shakes, the walls closing in, with reason enough, in my eyes at least reason enough, I blamed the sickness, drugs, for all of that.

But it was a sobering time, a time for thought and the pity is that I thought all wrong—I must have been still drinking, when I should have stopped. I could have stopped so easily then.

My last days in Madrid. Spain. Chaste. I had no woman nor money for a brothel. But peace of a sort. I sat at the bar and thought and drank, thought over my past and my try for a future. I thought I might go to Australia—a ten pound passage—start, if I could, a new life there.

The more I thought the more it seemed that Australia was the place for me.

Europe, what I had seen of it, was old, established and rich. You could make money, you could make a pile of money—the time was right then for making money—but you could, making fast money, as easily go to jail.

I had a fraud charge against me. I didn't know it, not then, but a fraud charge and a tax demand.

Australia, from what I'd read, seemed different. As though once there you were all equal—I was so naive, so wise in some things and yet naive. I thought of Australia as I had thought of London four years before—a kid, all ears, listening for a lion's roar, seeking a tent in Piccadilly Circus.

The night sky of Madrid, pulsing stars, a throbbing moon, and I sometimes walked and walked for miles in the relative cool of the midnight air. Thinking about Australia. I was to think of Australia for a long time as the great escape. It took years, all of the sixties and into the eighties before I discovered there was no escape, that you are what you are and are doomed with yourself.

A simple conclusion, it took nearly two decades and a devil chase, but I learned it.

And I still don't know myself.

Yet I thought to know myself in Madrid. My last days there. When, so young, my heart aches to think I was so young, so foolish, so tough yet weak—I could not pass a beggar—and what the fuck was I doing there, still there, in that city that almost killed me.

I did not leave it till I was out of money. So with a few pesetas I stood in the airport, waiting for a flight to London. It was the only flight. London. That day, or night, for the runway was all lit up as I left Madrid. Not to return. I have never seen Madrid again.

London.

Three times now I had been to that capital, another joint that had all but killed me, and in years to come would try again. And again. A fair effort, with help from me it would try again and again to kill me.

I came back from Spain with no gifts, nothing, not even brandy—I had shifted again to whisky, duty-free—Southern Comfort if I remember correct—and I had planned to go on to Jersey. Drunk I had thought to go on to Jersey. But there was no plane that night from that airport at that hour, and during the journey to town, this by now familiar town, I thought of going home to Glasgow.

Night train.

September. A definite chill. London. Night. Glasgow, morning, a positive cold. I shivered as I waited for a taxi.

I came home to a pile of mail, such letters, I never thought to be so popular, but shifting through them found a tax demand and for my ex-partner and I, that hard-faced crook, a charge of fraud.

It was pretty serious, jail serious and it took a lump of money to wriggle out.

I stalled on the tax. You do not, not usually, other than for evasion, go to jail for tax, but in the end I had to pay.

It left me broke, or almost, just some money here and there that guys had borrowed from me.

So I got a job. I went to work as a shunter for the

railway.

A few weeks on in the year, now 1965, I got a cheque for my car, the one stolen in London—I now had another—and the railway paid well—fake time-sheets and hours you had not worked, it would have been nearly impossible for any one man to have worked the hours that you claimed. But they paid you. You laid in bed and they paid you. And I was never short of a drink, you could get a drink at two in the morning free. There were other ways in my time with the railway in which I made it pay—I took some chances but made it pay and in the time I was there, built up on my savings.

That job with the railway was a gold mine. I made five or six times more money than the Station Master. I doubt that he was pleased and when I began to suffer black-outs, he set me up.

I made it easy for him.

As time went on I made it very easy for him.

I sacked myself.

The black-outs progressed. I would awake in the morning with no recall. It was a condition I was to learn to live with, as part, the price, of the drinking game. But first, as before, they were scary. I might be standing at a bar in all clarity, not drunk, or what I would have considered drunk, and have blacked-out in mid-sentence. So that I could remember a certain word, then nothing. Blackness.

I did not advertise this fact. Condition. And the guys that I drank with did not know. I know they did not know. I shunted trains in black-outs. Night shift. I would awake at say, three o'clock in the day and have no memory of the night before, of getting home.

Not always. I could get roaring drunk and still remember, but increasingly the black-outs struck.

The thing was that in those days I acted normal. By all accounts I acted normal, just a guy with a drink, half-drunk, and it was accepted then on the railway, at that shunting yard that you got half-drunk. But you were not supposed to put trains off the rails. For the first one, a train coming off the rails, a bad shock for the driver, I got a three-day suspension.

I appealed against it—sure, I'd had a drink, a couple of beers, but I was not drunk—and the thing was quashed.

But it was the beginning of the end of my time with the railway.

I was not upset, for I was sick of the job and the shifts, I liked the money but was sick of the job, and they—the Station Master and a few of his cronies—were sick of me.

Yet it is hard because of the union, at that time it was hard anyway, to get rid of a man. I should have been sacked a hundred times, the other guys fifty times, but, other than falling down, it is hard to prove that a man is drunk.

However, they knew of my drinking and my stealing and set a trap and caught me good.

It was my habit to take advantage of lulls and there were plenty of lulls, with no trains to shunt. When I would drink in pubs—the Railway Tavern or the Highland Fling. Some bosses and the railway police, the police by then had an interest in me, with the aid of a spy-glass, timed my drinking, my visits to the pubs.

I was presented with a document. I don't know how many signatures. It showed dates and times, my visits to the pubs.

I left the railway not badly off. I had made plenty for doing little, and I knew that with the interest of the cops it was best I left, for if caught that way I was not so sharp as I liked to think.

Booze.

It was hitting me now.

Stealing my wits.

And yet still I chose to ignore it.

I left the railway with something like two thousand pounds. Cash. A lot of money then in 1966. And a lot of ways, how I looked, I was in my prime. Booze it seemed just stole my wits. Then. I had yet to fall. I was as strong as a bull, steady-nerved, nothing jittery, not even in the mornings and with no shakes since Madrid. When I should have been failing I was blooming.

Just the black-outs, and these were minor compared to the ones to come. It was the cause of my fall, the delusion that I was different to the guys I knew, the Glasgow bums I saw, and I saw and knew a lot of bums.

All my life I have known a stack of bums.

Glasgow.

Manchester.

London.

Spain.

Sydney.

The list is long.

Places I've been.

But with two thousand pounds I left the railway. I had had more, at nineteen I had more money than at twenty-two, at twenty-nine I was a pauper compared to twenty-two, and at thirty-two I wished for twenty-nine, for the money that I had.

Bums.

I was on the way out aged thirty-two, and by thirty-three was even worse, wishing for the money, the smallest amount, that I had when thirty-two.

Still, with the two thousand pounds I visited Kabul in Afghanistan.

Amsterdam. I saw the advert—'Come to exciting Amsterdam'—and went, and went on with a gang of hippies, Americans, their destination Katmandu.

It is quite a jaunt from Amsterdam to Asia and in an old ambulance, all of us stoned, the wonder is that we made Kabul.

There were six of us including me who set out for the mountains of Nepal.

That time, that trip, *trips*—I was shifted into another

world, the new dimension of LSD—I do not regret for it was a fun time—at least to begin—and we set out from Amsterdam in late summer, late at night, in the old ambulance, three girls, and three boys, and peace and love and a bit too soon for the Flower Power of the following year.

Holland, flat straight roads, permissiveness—we should have stayed in Holland or Germany—there were bags of drugs and booze in Holland and Germany. But on we went, eastward, ever east, and for those kids, true innocents, all jeans and guitars, a journey to a nightmare.

One hippie died and the trip turned sour. Another, a boy, was raped, buggered, and after sundry adventures the party burst in Kabul, Afghanistan. The hippies who were still there, had come so far, flew—with wired money—home to America. I returned to Holland. It was much easier alone. At least I knew the score, what *could* happen. When I reached Amsterdam it was summer of the following year, July 1967.

If you are going to San Francisco be sure to wear a flower in your hair.

Every place, each bar and cafe you went to, walked past, that song, a classic of the time, memory of that time, and if in the East I had suffered a drought of booze—there were times and places during my time with the hippies when I was pushed for a drink—I hammered Dutch gin to make amends.

I stayed a couple of weeks in Amsterdam. In a hotel across from the Central Station. I liked the city, atmosphere, full of hippies, girls, new liberation, acting like boys—and not a few boys acting like girls—and it was the same, if less, in London when I got there.

If you are going to San Francisco be sure to wear a flower in your hair.

If ever a song caught the mood of the times.

Europe.

London.

Glasgow.

But Glasgow was dull compared to Europe or London, like another world compared to the East. A hard, cold city, violent—you are never in Glasgow far from violence—and not the place for a new generation if you wanted drugs or peace or to wear a flower in your hair.

Still it suited me and my legal dope, and again, in certain pubs I was a regular.

I went sometimes to wine-shops now, for I saw nothing wrong with wine. At sixteen years old I had seen nothing right about wine, but at twenty-three I saw it differently. Cheaper. More for less. But I was not, not then anyway, a wino. I just sometimes drank, got drunk on wine. And certainly I did not, as later, carry flagons home for through the night and morning drinking. Yet a taste for the grape—stuff that in the Manchester model after what I had seen—I had sworn I would never drink.

I was back to nothing, or almost. Just working, swinging a pick and shovelling stone, and as ever, if now with pick and shovel, I moved. I remember that winter, a very cold one, the coldest I've known, I worked in a camp in the far north of Scotland. Small difference between that place and Siberia, the moon in the mornings, hard bright stars, a cold rattled your teeth, burned your nose. Yet I liked it. I was off the booze in that place, all of the winter I was off the booze preparing for a bender in the spring.

Yet I thought, I was supposed to be saving as I swung my pick for a new life in Australia.

I worked November to April in that camp, and once more, after six months of work, I was not poor. And six months on the wagon, hard work, good food, the cleanest air, I was in the best shape of my life.

Coming home on the train to Glasgow, some three or four

guys and I shared a bottle of whisky. *White Horse*. They shared it out, passed it round, and when we made the city we went to the pub. A farewell drink. Whisky and beer. The first guy bought a round. It went to the next. We all bought a round, back again for the first guy to treat, and we were spending money, big calloused hands, broken nails, a winter of toil, as if there were no tomorrow.

Friday.

Saturday I was looking for more, for after that first drink, the drink on the train—tip from the bottle—I was hooked. I just could not, for weeks after, get enough. Of course the money went—six months of work, miser savings, went in six weeks or two months on the bottle.

It was a fierce affair when I hit the bottle. And drinking for nothing, no reason at all. I had dropped my shyness and was not backward. I could make-out in tough situations. And I could quit drinking. I had quit drinking for six months. Coming home on the train, if I had been alone I would not have drunk.

But I got drunk. Very. And it was a mean morning when I awoke, no recall, in Euston Station, London.

I was drinking for three or four weeks when I awoke in Euston Station.

The guard I think pushed me awake. Out of a drunken stupor. It was a surprise, a fright as I discovered where I was. And not knowing if I had bought a ticket and lost the ticket or travelled for free. In the event, last passenger, no ticket collector, I emerged out into the London morning.

Sad.

It is all I can say, sad, an ache I had never known existed in that station.

I went for a coffee. Stood. Waited. A morning in May. The queue was long. A noisy place, brightly lit, it hurt my head, my eyes, and worse, when I got the coffee, it came with a saucer, I shook so that I could not hold it.

I left the place, just walked away, across from the station, in Euston Road, next to a sex shop, to a liquor store which sold me a curer.

I bought a quarter bottle of whisky and a can of beer. The sun shone, a blue-sky morning, I crossed back to the station. The idea was to get the next train home. After a drink. I could not, how I felt, have bought a ticket, enquired about the train. Outside the station trying to drink. The first whisky I vomited up and the second was no better. And still I shook and still the sadness. The third one, a swig from the bottle, I managed to hold. It was an effort, sweat on my brow, a toe-curler, but I managed to hold it down. And the first one down, staying down, some swigs more I got to feeling better. Sitting on a wall outside of Euston Station.

I smoked, I could—I rolled my cigarettes—now make a smoke. Some tremor but nothing to before. And I was trying to remember last night in Glasgow. I could remember a pub, but the pub was in the Gorbals, far from the train station, I had had no thought of coming here. Still I consoled myself that it was better than jail, where after those bouts on other mornings, I had awoken. I had awoken in jail, in a cell, much as I had awoken in London on a train. The only difference in London, other than freedom, was that it was the first time since Madrid that I had shaken. That and a sadness that I can't explain, its extent, all the woe of the world: a crashing tide, wave after wave, as if an endless sea, until I drank the whisky.

And I drank the whisky, it was so easy now the first one was down and staying down—but I felt the shame of my shakes and drinking now, in the morning in the open, outside of Euston Station. If I had had no whisky I could have wept, sat down and cried.

But the booze soon blunted my shame, rid me of my despair. It got me feeling that well, that I was in London and might as well make the best of it.

Yet I wondered at my sadness, such an incredible ache,

no cause—I truly saw no cause in my sadness. But cheering a bit, near to my usual self, I thought about a bit of fun, a night on the town, before I went home.

I had money and was not badly dressed for a night on the town, and how I saw it, after my journey—had I paid the fare?—I was entitled to some fun, a night on the town.

The more I thought—work-hardened hands, a winter of toil, no booze—I was entitled to all the fun that I could get.

Not an hour on and in from the lowest I had ever been and I thought about fun, merriment, and could hardly wait for the London night. But more, I think, I wanted to forget.

The morning past, I bought more booze and was very drunk when the pubs all opened, and afterwards with a blue-black negress, frizzled hair, big brass ear-rings, in a room I know not where, I hammered wine and hammered her, who thinking me sleeping, tried to rob me.

I hit her high on the left temple. I know it was the left temple for I felt the pain in my right fist. A punch as hard, drunk or sober, as any I had ever thrown. She fell in a heap. I sat on the bed and drank the wine and looked at her who might be dead. Crazy? I was mad. Sitting on that bed drinking the wine and proud the punch had felled her. A big woman, big thighs, big feet. Splayed. White. I remember the white soles of her feet as I remember my pride at the punch had felled her. Like she was a man. In a crummy room, I sat on the bed and thought of robbing her.

Thankfully she stirred to rise and sat on the bed (there were no chairs) and moaned in *fear*, real fear in her big white blood-shot eyes, the madman—I might have been fucking Mr Hyde who she had tried to rob.

At her fear and her eyes—and I was of a mind to thrash her further, with righteousness I thought to thrash her further—I was moved to compassion. Sadness. This woman. Who was not young, huge sagging breasts, for whom the struggle must be hard, and I was sorry to have hit her. Yet she showed some spirit, sign of fight, she had even complained. I dread to think what might have been.

As it was I was moved, drunk but ashamed—such sudden, swinging moods—and moved close to press against her.

I remember it all, that day in that room, with the finest clarity: I can remember almost word for word that day in that room.

'You shouldn't have tried tae rob me.'

Her head was swollen, a fist-sized lump, and she looked so ugly, old and vulnerable, it was all I could do not to beg her blessing.

'I'll give you money.'

I could smell her smell, woman, musk and decay, and I would have given her all my money just to have her smile, a wink to me.

'I'm sorry.'

We sat back, nudists both. I don't know if we had some sex or merely tried for sex.

I drank some wine. 'But you shouldn't have tried tae rob me.'

'I'm sorry.'

'Then we're both sorry.'

'I've *nothing*,' she said.

'I'm not a rich man.'

'But a kind one.'

'I do my best.'

'I know that, love.'

'What's your name?'

'Bessie.'

'Are you married, Bessie?'

'I was but he left me.'

'Then he was a fool.'

We shared the wine. Metallic. It tasted metallic. Thin. I can taste it now, that stuff, full bottles in a plastic bag, that I could not remember buying.

I touched Bessie's head. 'My God, I didn't mean it!'

'I deserved it.'

'Does it hurt?'

'But I've been hit worse. For nothing I've been hit worse.'

'You're a brave girl, Bessie.'

'But I don't like to be hit on the head.'

'I won't hit you again.'

'I know you won't, love.' Then, looking at me with big red-shot eyes, 'I'm really an honest woman, I'm poor but I'm honest.'

'I know you are.' Sitting on the edge of the bed. 'And a fine figure of a woman too.' Such rot, shit, such a drunken fool, and from she to me, as vengeance, a dose of the clap. After. In Glasgow. When something like sane I thought to be mad, on a night on the town.

I had a sore dick and a sore head on my visits to Black Street, the clinic there. And attending the clinic, it was the first time I thought about my drinking. For I knew that with no booze I wouldn't have been in London, and—after that room in London—a great remorse that lasted days.

But a short memory, the money alone, six months of work, hard work, I'd blown. Behaviour I would sooner forget.

I hated that I had hit a woman. With all my heart I hated that I had hit a woman, whore or not, and even with the pox I hated that I had hit a woman. In truth I think it kept me drinking, although it should have stopped me drinking. But it was more easy to take, forget, when I'd had a few. The whole affair, the morning, my shakes in the station, drinking outside the station and the towering sadness, I wished to forget.

And I was forgetting, just a week or two I suffered, and then as always, as on my very first drunk, what had loomed a horror boomed a laugh.

I thought as I got over my shame that it was no great disaster. That woman, the pox, the money I'd blown. It was nothing lasting and I had no problem making money. If I now worked, dug holes for my money, I had no problem making it. Not as much as I'd have liked but, working, and I worked long hours, saved me from the bottle. And from excess of booze it saved me. For a time. For again, with an eye to Australia, I had begun to try to save.

The puzzlement of booze, when I returned from London, and I returned in a dream—as if on a magic carpet—I had no shakes, no sadness. I was sorry, I regretted London, it was no joke that I had the pox, but no true sadness— nothing like in Euston Station on the morning of my despair.

So I forgot the thing, just one of those things, and after a few weeks at home, my mother's house, I was working again.

At Glasgow Cross or Gorbals Cross I used to pick up the truck and ride out with a gang of labourers, on the open back. I was doing, repeating with little difference, what my father had done in the days of my childhood.

But I was still young—I could get drunk, sleep all night behind the door, and never miss a shift.

I had thoughts of course for a better life, some notion of being a concert promoter, but with Australia in mind it seemed not worth the effort.

So I just worked and drank, saved what I could and again, some years away, made visits to the library.

Regrets? I had a past, but it was too short, and thinking of Australia I was too eager for a future. I doubt whether I had any regrets aged twenty-four. What had been was dead and gone and I was not the sort to worry. It took a hell of a lot to worry me when I was twenty-four. London, my shakes, sadness, my stay with Bessie, and a stay of days, had shook me to consider booze, to think about my drinking, but not enough to worry me. There was a lot in my life that should have worried me, some fights I was in, my drop from boss to worker, but I could sit at nights, content, with a book. When not out drinking I could sit at night contented with a book.

A new library now got my custom. And on visits there I first met Jean, the girl I recollected with the start of all this, my debauch in Barcelona.

She knew I drank but not how I drank. I was on our first nights out, too anxious to impress. She, blonde, pert, just seventeen, stirred a tender feeling in me. I did not want to hurt her.

But my missing days, time in the brothel, fucked-up holiday.

For what, the months I'd known her, Jean had saved. From her first trip abroad, to return with the clap, and that Spanish dose was a rampant one.

And yet, as I said, I laughed. Later I laughed at the memory.

At twenty-five I still was blind. I could see in booze, the creature I became, but could not, looking at other guys and how they drank, see myself for different. They drank, I drank. All my life, all the men I had known, they all took drink. It is no crime, drunkenness, and definitely not in Glasgow. A working man in Glasgow is expected to drink. The men I knew, guys I worked with, most of them, continued static with a given amount or were only drunk at weekends. I was different—well, I saw that we were different, that I was bolder, like it was a stronger load that I could carry. I only saw a good way that we were different. A few drinks in I saw it better than good that we were different. But not in the mornings. Hangovers were sore things now. And I had to work, dig roads. I could not, because of my drinking, save a penny, for my dream of Australia was still a ten pounds passage and I couldn't risk a prison cell.

It is some clue as to my drinking then that what money I

earned—and this was money enough for the other men, married men, to keep their families on, to go on holiday—did not pay my booze bill.

Looking back on those days and I was not stupid—I was addled but not stupid—it might have been that I thought of Australia as a cure for my habit. A new start. I was grasping at straws.

This was the summer of 1969. A desperate one, I was a desperate man—but my luck was good and I had the money for Australia.

Brisbane.
Sydney.
Townsville.

I did not like Australia. I liked Bondi Beach, the ladies there, but it is shit, Australia, the Australian male, the big tough man he likes portrayed. There were tough men, but not the toughest. That distinction, one on one, I'd give to the navvies, the guys I worked a winter with.

Arriving in Australia I had in my head thoughts of the toughest men, the hardest drinkers and fighters, a place, a land like the early days of the American West. Which it was not. No. A city, Sydney, just like London, if mostly white, they had something of a colour bar in Australia at that time. And being a city like London, which I considered bad luck, I hated it. But I had little money, I had to work. And knowing no one, with no trade or skill, I was soon back to pick and shovel.

I never rose in Australia from my work with a pick and shovel, and the sad truth is that for the work I did I could have earned more in Scotland.

And I drank.

And always, the long week starting, just waiting for Friday, pay-day, when with no work on Saturday I would get especially drunk. The whole thing, twelve thousand miles, daily toil, weekend drunks, was a total waste. Indeed I was never so sure in Australia, and after my first week there, to have made a mistake.

Had I money enough I would have gone home. My first week there I would have gone home. But I had to stay. Work first, dig the roads of Sydney as I had dug the roads of Glasgow and London. And always waiting for Friday, living hand to mouth and always waiting for Friday.

There were good times. There had to be good times, but on the whole it was a mean two years I squandered in Australia.

Looking back, thinking now about the stages in my life, if I had first hit London two years too soon I made it to Australia two years too late.

I was crippled by my drinking. I lived and worked for the bottle all the time I was there. It had me in a devil's choke. I was with no money on the streets in the cities of Australia, but a simple slip, a fractured bone, removed from a hobo, a meths-drinking bum.

My hangovers, though I could shake them, were corkers now. *Shakes.* It was not only my hands but my poor head shook. I shuffled in the mornings like a punchy boxer. And it took longer now with no proper food and the cheap plonk I drank, to throw them off.

It was the first serious time, with these hangovers and always poor, that I thought about quitting, giving up drinking. I thought every Monday morning about giving up, but I couldn't, and on a Friday with my pay in my pocket I would start. Even aware of the Monday and how low I would feel.

I had the poke, sweats, shakes, but mercifully, I missed the horrors in Australia. Where I met with a girl who in a twist of my life, was to be unforgettable.

She was German, blue-eyed and blonde. Heidi. I went first with her sister, older, a nurse, and it amazes me still, from the women I've known, the female attraction to drunkards. As though it's a challenge to reform them.

It must be something like that but they don't have a hope.

Still, when I first met Heidi, I was fit and lean and hard after a trip and I suppose I was attractive to women.

I had met with the sister on Bondi beach but from the first, it was Heidi that I wanted.

My times outback, beet-cutting, and they paid you well if you hacked all day, swung a machete from dawn till dusk. I had money and more to go home after some months. But I blew it, had a ball, or what I thought was a ball, in Sydney. So it was not all poverty and waiting till Friday, if looking back now on Sydney or Melbourne, Brisbane, it seems that way.

I will finish with Australia, for to continue would read more like a tale of adventure, an adventurer, than the heartbreak run of a very sick man.

Adventurer no. I was never an adventurer, my only sober, healthy run of adventure, could you call it that, when I was fifteen years old and first went to London. The rest of the stuff was just thoughts of escape, as if to rid myself of a sickness, creeping, the stealth of a snake, that I did not understand.

It ended in Australia, Sydney, with an affair with Heidi (the sister then with a new man-friend) that I took for casual, and her attractions were not enough to keep me there, in a land I thought, from those glossy brochures of a wonderful life, had hoodwinked me into coming.

I had robbed to go to Australia and as I had to pay full fare back—I robbed to get out.

I arrived in London, Heathrow, an embittered, not nice man. A failure. It rankled. I had been better off in this city at sixteen years old. Eleven years ago. At least then I had *hope*, and was a much nicer boy then than I was now as a man.

Yet I was not, not this time, drunk in London. I could still stop drinking. At times in Australia, the outback, beet-cutting, I had to stop drinking as there was no drink to drink, and the job was too tough to do hungover. My problem was I could not stay stopped.

It took all of my money and almost my life to stay stopped—but that happy state was a long way distant as I arrived in Heathrow Airport. Yet I knew at Heathrow, as I had known in Australia and before Australia, in Barcelona, that there was something far wrong with the way I drank, my behaviour drunk.

But alcoholic, alcoholism—you told me that I'd have punched your nose.

Then.

Twenty-seven years old. I reasoned I *could* stop. Just like all the way, during the flight from Australia, I had been dry. It was what threw me. I supposed an alcoholic was a guy not able to stop, or stop with free money in his pocket. I associated alcoholism with London, the bums who slept in Waterloo Station. Or Manchester, Glasgow, Sydney, where guys lived rough, with two coats on and bushy beards. And a lot of other men have been fooled by the same idea.

But in Heathrow, well-heeled, a good watch, good suit, and sober all the way, I had a drink in the airport lounge.

Why not? I had a little money.

I went to Ireland.

Why?

I don't know.

Dublin.

There are plenty of pubs in Dublin, all-day pubs, or shut for just one hour but, after a while, on a drunken whim, I thought I'd visit a cousin in Cork.

Now this guy, this cousin, I had seen him just once, and then when I was just a kid, both of us kids in short pants.

But I was in Ireland and thought I'd surprise him. A fleeting visit, and found myself on the bus to Cork—where, and a surprise to me, I saw the bird-like man who had clutched his ears in the dentist's in Madrid.

The bus was no express. It stopped with an amazing frequency, and always at each stop was a pub, where with a like frequency, I was mistaken for my cousin Shaun, a wild one who was just out of jail after some years in an English prison.

So it was a party in Cork, where I walked the streets and people called me Shaun.

I stayed with my cousin and his mother, who both of them took a drink, and at Shaun's party, liberation, I drank as heavily as I have ever drunk—and I don't know how long I stayed, a week or a month—but when I got back to Dublin I was ill. A sense of imbalance, queer tingle in my fingertips. It was alarming, the tingle. A fear with each step I took that I might fall. I consulted a doctor, who was fat as a fool with all the fast look of a Buddha, snug and content—and a good drink in him—and he told me to lay off the booze.

'That's a tall order.'

'Or,' he said, 'drink just Guinness—Guinness is the great body-builder.'

The look of him, his smell of booze—Guinness I fancied—it would seem to be so.

But he gave me vitamins and I took his advice. It was no hardship, you could get drunk on Guinness: it took a few pints but you could get good and drunk on that heavy black brew.

I got back to Scotland, Glasgow, where I continued the treatment, drank Guinness with a will. But feeling such a failure. I saw my old partner, with a fine house, Mercedes car and I felt a bum. No malice in my old partner, I felt like a bum. Without him, his car and house, I still would have felt a bum, having no house, no car, dwindling money, staying with my mother.

I went back to labouring. It was all I knew. My only sure way of making money. But what money I made I drank. I paid my mother my keep and drank the rest. In many ways, how I lived, I was not unlike Edward, the uncle who had lived upstairs. In many ways in Glasgow I was not unlike a lot of men. Working to drink, living to die. No aspirations, way out, or drinking, wanting a way out.

Truly it was booze, and the more I write, the more of a riddle it is. Habit? It is much more than that. All the pull of narcotics, a true addiction. Yet as you suffer and you see a doctor, most doctors do not want to know. No. And I have met a lot of doctors, too many to mention, to list one by one.

And yet even with the eyes of a child—as I had viewed Edward—there is something all wrong in the man who will forfeit, say, shoes for bottles of booze.

That I went further, forfeited much more the sicker I was, the luckier I am I can tell the tale.

But back from Australia, Ireland, and again with my mother and again with a pick and shovel, at nights I was skint and went back to visits to the library.

I began with Jack London and Hemingway—reading short stories. The form impressed me, sharp and tight and you could read a few, several adventures in a night. And I was so impressed that I began to write short stories. There was a trick, the art, and at nights with a bottle of wine, I got sleepy and drunk and badly frustrated.

But it was the closest in my life I had come to a hobby, if soon, with nightly efforts, it became more of an obsession. Short story writing. Bottle of wine drinking. I had little time for anything else. Trying to type, and I forget what was the hardest, the writing of the stories or trying to type them.

The first one I sold, to a girlie magazine, I got ten guineas for. I remember it yet, my feeling, wonder that I had sold a story, which was not a very good story, but rather than encourage me it finished me writing.

It was like I had proved something. Fuck knows what, and I drank, bought wine with the money. I continued to read but stopped writing. For a year at least I stopped writing. And because of my drinking, for I had not stopped that, I went to jail on one-night stands—for by now, I was falling down—many times.

I would awake in jail cells, and had come to accept jail cells, as during my days with the railway I had accepted the black-outs, as part of the price of the drinking game.

And yet I worked. I would sometimes go direct to work from jail, a night in a cell, for I was scared to lose the shift and the booze it could buy.

At twenty-seven, twenty-eight years old, it was the true beginning of my years of torture.

I won a bet, a roll-up on the horses, six horses, which came close to a thousand pounds.

It was a surprise that I won this bet, one Saturday, and it was Sunday before I thought to check it.

On Monday I did not go to work.

The bookie had not got the money on hand and we went to the bank, where a big-eyed teller paid me out my winnings.

It is a fair roll, one thousand pounds in ten pound notes.

I was working, swinging a pick, clearing at that time about twenty-five or thirty pounds a week. And I was able to drink, get drunk, stagger to a fall and end in jail, on that. With this new money, like El Dorado—the name incidently, El Dorado, of a wine I drank—I soon shifted back to whisky. Black Label. Or brandy. Napoleon. And drinking it, after some days of drinking it, I arrived again in London.

Abruptly, as before, only this time drunk, too drunk for the shakes or for sadness, and with a bottle of whisky to keep me high, it was not the nightmare of my stay with Bessie.

During this stage of my drinking, and it was verging on the crucial, or past the crucial (I contradict for I do not know) it was a relief to wake free in London with a bottle of whisky. Rather than no whisky, no nothing, or only the shakes in a Glasgow police cell.

I had plenty of money, my passport, and went on a wild trip to Paris and Rome, travelling light, just a pair of jeans, some shirts and a toothbrush.

I returned to Glasgow after five weeks at most. I had a scar (a knife-fight in Rome) and a beard and nothing else.

Skint.

Broke.

Fucked.

Sick.

No job.

Nothing.

I had to borrow from my mother.

One thousand pounds, or almost.

I wished I'd never won it.

It took days after that orgy before I could eat again.

Two days or three before I could shave, even clip my beard and when I did it showed a shocker. Grey. Thin. Sharp-nosed, long-toothed. I was surprised by the length of my teeth, like a death's head staring back at me.

That was the physical side of what booze had done in Paris and Rome, Glasgow and London. Mentally, such remorse, as breathing dead, no spirit or fight; it was even worse.

The bastard stuff was stealing my soul. I lay in bed, lethargic, a beaten body, a body with its needs and lusts that I had come to despise—my tortured head, I despised my body and its demands upon me. It was the lowest I had been. I would speak to no one. My whole life, being, a total void. Nothing. Or only sadness. But not knowing what I was sad about. The thousand pounds, it had come and gone, it did not really bother me. My job, I could get another. My health, my body would heal, my face would fatten, good colour return. What I had done, and some shameful things, they were over and past. But the sadness, welling up, I could not understand the sadness. Booze, stuff, was supposed to have you jolly.

It was all wrapped up, they were locked, the booze and my sadness.

Yet if I did not want the sadness I did not want to quit on booze.

Even then, at my lowest ebb, I could not see a life without drink. And as time passed by I forgot the knife-fight, my beard—a tramp's beard, verminous underwear, sweats and shakes and all the rest. Except the sadness. I was concerned enough about the sadness to consider my drinking. With a few drinks in me, nothing drunk but a few drinks in me, I approached Alcoholics Anonymous.

I did not, not then, consider myself an alcoholic. I was fit again and working and I could stop drinking. All of four days, Monday to Friday, I could stop drinking. But my trip through Europe, Paris and Rome, my knife-fight in Rome, the sadness on my return that I could not finger, I did not want that again.

I would have preferred some other agency than Alcoholics Anonymous—it sounded so desperate, but the anonymity bit appealed to me.

I went, and strangely after all that I had drunk, I went to learn how to drink.

It was my purpose for my visit to that place, a run-down hall beneath a railway track in Cunningham Street, Glasgow.

First guy I met inside the joint was the one-eyed guy I had worked with and had sometimes drunk with in the wino haunt that had sold cheap cider, in our long-ago days in the beast-feed place. He welcomed me with open arms.

I felt embarrassed at the place, the guys around seated at tables. A hall now gone as he has gone, dead. Victim to the bottle. A good guy. It is a fact, that booze, in my experience, from a cross-section of men I have known, takes a lot of the good ones. It certainly took my one-eyed friend who that day seemed a picture of health, robust and strong and everything, with a wife, young family, kids he adored, to live for. But he drank, and drinking, unable to stop, he died.

It is a classic story, about a million times a classic story. I was to meet at AA quite a few guys that I used to know. But none more tragic than my one-eyed pal. Who called me Mick, and said 'This is the place tae be.'

I wondered at the shape of the hall, ramshackle, the guys, some hobos, who hung about there. This was at about six or seven at night—the place was open all day—before the meeting at eight. But it was good to see a guy I knew, and we swapped stories, and I remember thinking, clearly I remember thinking, that it was a pity that he could not drink.

Still he did come with me and I had a couple before the meeting. I think that he came with me when I went back. It is like that at AA, a *caring* fellowship. You will get help. That my pal died, that for many years I continued to drink, is no fault of AA. My pal had many good years sober and in my case I could not admit booze had me licked.

Pride?

Shame?

Shit.

I wanted to drink.

I was looking for a way to drink.

That visit, meeting, and for many meetings, I had no intention of quitting, or trying to quit. There is nothing short of death if you think that way, that anyone can do. I wanted to drink. I wanted my wits but obviously I wanted drink more.

At my first meeting in that place in Cunningham Street I sat in the front row and was not impressed. I will not give the formula, one day at a time, or go into the format of AA meetings. But there were people who smoked like chimneys, never have I met such smokers, who spoke of a Higher Power, a God as they understood him, and the enormous danger (so true) of the first drink, first *step* and that we (they tended to speak and address the company as a whole) were powerless over alcohol.

I liked the people, the one-eyed guy, but it was not the first drink that brought me there. And all the time at that meeting they hammered on about the first drink. Which of course meant no drink. There was other stuff, some flowery talk, but it counted for nothing—in my eyes it counted for nothing, no drink.

That place, those people, just advocates of temperance—it stuck in my craw, I took a resentment to the idea of no drink, not even a spoonful, even if deep-down I knew it was true.

So true that I wanted nothing more to do with that place, those people who for all their talk, first step or first drink, boasted some active drunks within the ranks.

After the meeting the place sold coffee in cracked mugs. They were kind people—without exception the people were kind, you do not feel a stranger long in AA—and I have not done justice to that dump. I don't know what I had expected but I had some idea that doors worked, opened and closed the wrong way round, like had you pulled you should have pushed. Inside the place was big as a church, so that, if I had been sober, a genteel drunk, I'd fancy it a fright. And it might well be that that place served its purpose, scared many a man to change his ways. I'd seen better and cleaner models, night-shelters, but some men I know a few, got sober and stayed sober in that place.

The end of the meeting, drinking the coffee, and even the coffee was rotten, I got invited to other meetings.

'They're not all like this.'

But even if it did not stop me drinking, like with the

boxing at the gym in Dennistoun, I fitted into that place. I went back a few times. I made a few pals. The building is demolished now.

I told no one of my flirt with Alcoholics Anonymous, and drinking with no change, gave no reason to suspect.

A dual life continued for a while, until disillusioned, given the order not to drink, rather than give up booze I gave up on the meetings.

But there was no fun in drink. It had long since ceased —my first days in London perhaps, some quirk in my first visit to Paris—to be any fun.

Yet I continued to partake. I don't know why or I could not stop, even though I thought I was able to stop. I did stop. Three days of no money, Tuesday to Friday, I did not drink. But I suffered on those days for the four I had drank. It was no way to live. Such an effort to get out of bed. Mondays, after the weekend session, were especially grim. The world was black on Mondays. I needed a curer on Monday mornings, to ward off the shakes to lunchtime and night would taper them off.

Winter.

The moon in the mornings.

Stars.

My mother served me tea in bed.

I dreaded the day.

Long, bleak hours, and the Monday dawned when I could not go to work, face the day.

It became regular on Monday mornings that I could not face the day, and soon, for now I was drinking all day Monday, Tuesday was the same.

I was trapped in a vicious circle, not able to work, no money—and I needed a lot of money.

It is neither here nor there, not now, it is sufficient that I had an eye for a chance and that I was not afraid to take a chance.

Whatever, for a while, no work to do and money in my pocket, I drank as a gent of leisure.

But by the way I drank, and now I was drinking wine by choice, I was no gent.

Wine.

I drank it all day and night and through the night. Lanliq and El Dorado. There was, for I could not sleep, always a bottle by my bedside. Lanliq or El Dorado. I found it easier when I awoke from a doze, like three or four in the morning, to drink wine than spirits. I could, after a couple of belts of the stuff, go back to sleep, or doze but the insomnia, drink induced, was getting me down enough to visit the doctor for some sleeping pills.

At first I was put on Mogadon and Doridon, hypnotics, but they did not work so I progressed to barbiturates, Nembutal.

The prescribed dose was two a night, the same as the hypnotics, and in my attempts to get some sleep I had been overdosing on the hypnotics, with no ill-effects but no sleep either, and thought—as a matter of course—to do the same with Nembutal.

Well, in short, I slept. I slept and I was lucky to awaken. About ten o'clock the following night. I was alone in the house, I forget where my mother was, but I do not, still drugged, forget my stagger to the closet. It was my habit to have a piss in the sink, the hand-basin, and in a mirror above the hand-basin, a glimpse, a shock, my lips showed white.

It was the first time in weeks when awakening that I did not think of wine. It took all of my effort to make some coffee. I was drugged but shaken and dreadfully weary. I thought to walk, thought that I should walk, but after some mugs of coffee I went back to bed.

I awoke again about three in the day. The dope was wearing off. I felt much better, some power in my limbs. I went for a piss and there was some colour in my lips. Yet still I sighed.

I went back to bed.

A more natural sleep this time, to awake at midnight.

This time, my piss, my lips showed normal. I had a raging hunger, and in the early hours had a monster meal, still with no thought of wine and I had plenty of wine to equal my monster slumber.

It had been a close call no doubt, and another couple of pills could have been the end of me. But I felt good, fed and rested, better than I had felt for months, cleansed of booze, nothing hungover, and with a look at the pills, capsules, bright-yellow, I thought to see a way to an end to drunkenness. Those things, they had you out, and if I could juggle the dose, sleep say twelve or fourteen hours, there would be no through-night booze, and then something like normal drinking.

I was so desperate and troubled by my drinking to cut half of my life away.

I ran a bath and shaved my beard—I felt like Rip Van Winkle as I shaved my beard.

But no drink, no shakes.

I sat in my pyjamas, a dressing-gown with a glass of wine and a smoke. I felt due a glass of wine. And enjoying my smoke. I was up on cigarettes to a hundred a day. I saw my smoking as all the more reason why I slept so deeply. Long. But not too long. It was a question of juggling the pills.

Sitting drinking the wine, low music and peace of a sort, the first for months.

There were letters and newspapers to read from my days in the coma.

Reading, drinking, some glasses of wine, some Nembutal. When I opened my eyes again I had a beard.

It was day-time, only I had missed a day. And I was hungover this time, stiff in the joints and again white-lipped. After almost a week of it now, two sleeps, I knew it was no good.

I had no intention of dying, and drunk, then drugged on those fucking pills, had come close twice.

It was night before I surfaced, felt fit to rise, to wash and shave.

And I still was tired.

Enough was enough of this remedy, and I got rid of the pills. But in days to come I would go back to them.

The drinking continued, the wine. I was now done with what flirt I had had with AA. I heard of the death of my one-eyed pal. It did not impress me. Either way that he had died, or I chose to think, the failure of AA, it did not impress me. It was AA members who told me about his death though, and I was impressed by their sincerity, hope for me. I who had given up hope, who could see no life without the bottle, only the bastard was that there was little life with the bottle. I was caught in a vortex. There were the usual fights, nights in jail, and now visits to priests—solemn oaths that I would drink no more, and sometimes that same day, just hours after, I would drink again.

Yet despite my drinking my appearance held, and somehow I was still strong and weighing the same as when I was twenty. If you saw me dressed—or undressed for that matter and you did not know me, you would never have known the booze I had guzzled. And I still went with ladies: I was no bum. To look at I was no bum.

The ladies (and there were some honeys) toothless hags, not always, but sometimes on drunken nights when I awoke there were toothless hags to frighten you. I miss a lot of detail, but the general picture is there, if as yet no horrors, just one of wine and drunkenness, loneliness, I was terribly lonely, and even more so in a crowd.

The phone rang.
'Hullo.'
'Michael?'
'Speaking.'

'It's me, Heidi.'
I had to think.
'Australia,' she said. 'Sydney.' Then, 'Remember?'
'You're in Sydney?' My head was blocked.
'No,' she laughed. 'London—but you remember me?'
'Of course I remember you.'
'I thought' she said, 'you might have forgotten.'
'You're kidding.'

Next day was full of memories of her, long and golden, summer in Sydney, Bondi Beach, and I was on the London train.

It was May 1973.

I had little money, I think just fifty or sixty pounds, but I wanted to see her.

She met me at the station, Euston and it was different this time, there at that station with someone to meet me, and I was sober. Very sober, no drink at all. Meeting her, who from Australia knew I drank if not quite how I drank. She was tall and slender, no change, not even her smell, her perfume, as I felt her softness press against me. It was the beginning of a heartache, a terrible time, but I had no way to know that when I met Heidi in Euston Station. She dressed casual, washed jeans and sneakers. I wore a suit. It was the first and the last time that she saw me in a suit. We went for lunch.

About one, two o'clock. I had got the seven-five train, a fast one from Glasgow.

We talked, laughed about Australia, shared a bottle of wine, and if I had liked or lusted after her in Sydney, I was now a little older and found how to care in London. Sitting, laughing, eating, drinking wine—but good wine, dinner stuff not the Glasgow rot-gut, jungle juice, that I partook of. I asked her how she got my number.

'You were the third Michael Thorn that I rang.'

'Then third time lucky.'

'There were only three Thorns in the book.'

'I thought you were still in Australia.'

'I've been home nearly a year.'

'Then you should have phoned me before.'

'I thought to—'

'You should have.'

'This is my first time in London.'

'Alone?'

'With you,' she said, 'I thought.'

'You're not going back to Australia?'

'I don't know.'

'No?'

'I'm not sure.'

'Your sister?' I asked.

'She's still there—she's married now.'

'I thought that she might be.'

'You left,' she said, 'Australia awful sudden.'

'My father was sick.'

'You didn't say.'

'I had no time.' I was not a bad liar. Christ, I had plenty of experience, from some of the things I'd done, fixes I'd been in, I had to be a good liar.

'He's all right now?'

'He's dead.'

'I'm sorry.'

'It's long ago.'

'It's not,' she said, 'too long ago.'

'No.' I smiled. She was conscious of her age, but I knew she was not yet twenty-two. 'I thought,' I said, 'that you would be married.'

'No,' she said with a smile, 'not yet.'

We ate, drank the wine, I ordered another bottle of wine—with Heidi, a girl I'd had and wanted again. It was, with her the first affection for a very long time. A good feeling, a feeling I'd almost forgotten in the life I led, guys I knew in my wild and drunken days. Now I wanted some tenderness. I did not love her, I would never love her, but I was fond enough of her to be protective, and to feel something like a man again.

I was so far gone so brutal were my thoughts, addled with booze, animal my reaction.

But sober then. Considerate. Kind. I tried to be considerate. Kind. While telling her a bag of lies, that in Glasgow I was doing grand—for suddenly I was afraid to lose her, as if she were my last stab at happiness.

We had a good few days. Walking. Eating. Laughing. Even if I had to sell my watch, a Rolex, about all of value I had in the world, to play out my stupid brag and rich act. But in the mornings, she with me, sweet tangle, dewy, in sleep the face of a child, trusting—the horrors of my recent past were well worth the Rolex. I don't regret the Rolex. And I don't regret those days in London. Now. Though, and not so long ago, I cursed them and her for all my trouble.

Idyllic days, nights, a walk in Hyde Park where I proposed.

I worried, it crossed my mind about the money needed for my marriage, in Germany, a town on the Rhine, but I thought that love or what passed for it would find a way.

And the bastard is it would if I hadn't got drunk.

Heidi didn't care that I had no money. I met her father—who had money—and neither did he.

I returned from that visit to London, the first happy one, with great hopes for the future.

I had by this time, after renewed efforts at writing, spasmodic, published a few short stories. I had them published here and there though mostly in the *Glasgow Herald*. Saturday issues. Some were good, and some not so good but on the strength of them the Scottish Arts Council saw fit to award me five hundred pounds.

I had not thought to win this prize. So it was a pleasant surprise, a bit of prestige, and I thought about a holiday. Alone. Like a final fling as a single man, so I went to Ibiza.

June.

The plan was that Heidi and I, we would be married in July.

Indeed in Germany, the town on the Rhine, the preparations for my marriage were already advanced.

But I went to Ibiza. I was not sober as I boarded the plane, for a week—or I thought a week—in the sun.

I was as drunk as a coot when I landed on that island. My second visit to a place of cheap wine, light and shadow, strong brandy, where the next day I awoke in a bed in a hotel in San Antonio where for the life of me I could not remember checking in. Little surprise, as I could not remember landing on the island. But knowing I was going it was not the shock I had when I first arrived, with no memory and no intention of going, in Euston Station, London.

I awoke around noon. It was hot. Very. The hotel was fine, big and modern, a swimming pool, a bar—the bar beside the swimming pool, blue water, and lots of people loafing, sunning, drinking there. I joined them. I drank. I was, with the five hundred pounds from the Arts Council given to assist me as a writer, on a bender. No breakfast, coffee, nothing, not even shaved, I sat by the pool and drank the brandy.

It would have been easy in that place, by that pool, to pick up a girl, but I was not interested in girls, only booze—by fuck what a pull in that stuff that stole my head. It is why booze in my mind is much more than habit, for I did not want to get drunk, yet drinking, I knew I would get drunk.

Full glasses I drank, brandy and beer and still sitting in last night's wear. I hadn't shaved, what chance had I to change my clothes? And again, that crowded pool was so lonely, each glass I drank was more lonely, and drinking, still drinking as the moon came up, a wonderful moon—or it might well have been the dropping sun—it is all I remember of that day.

Next day, and still nothing to eat, not even coffee to drink, I was again drinking by the pool, feeling even more lonely in a place, the dames around, where there was no need to be lonely, had I not been drinking I would have been far from lonely—and I telephoned Germany. Heidi. It was the biggest mistake. I asked her out, begged her to come join me, under the night sky of Spain, and she came, joined me in Ibiza.

It was a fiasco from the start, I was on a bender that I could not stop, slow down, morning and night and through the night, not eating or shaving—I kidded to be growing a beard—or washing. When I tried to have a wash, a shower, I was either too drunk or had a dose of the jitters. Drinking brandy and heavy sweet wine. A truly, even my standards, gargantuan bout. I tried to drink that island dry. And I had the hire by then, hair-raising rides, twisting roads, of a motor scooter. I had a case full of clothes but wore, and wore all the time, just jeans and a tee-shirt. Filthy. In a flashy hotel. I had words with the manager over my behaviour and language (some guests had complained). I took offence and we moved out, bag and baggage, the motor scooter in the middle of the night, and for Heidi this was not the man she had known in London.

But I could not stop drinking, even in moments of sanity, sobriety, I could not stop drinking. I knew I was losing her and could not stop drinking. And now I was sorry she was there, for I was not lonely at all and I thought I had been mad for asking, begging her out.

We shifted to a hotel, a hippy joint, in Ibiza Town. It was about the only place that would have me in, where there were other guys, quite a few, who grew beards and did not wash. But Heidi was no hippy, a smart chic, hip, but nothing hippy. And it was a mean time for her in a room with me, a king hippy; a bout on the brandy and wine, perhaps with the help of the sun, that turned me to an animal.

The truth is that during that bout she was a pest. Woman to be my wife. I smile at it now, those days, the woman to be my wife. And yet it hurts. But I couldn't stop drinking and each day I was more wild with a total disregard for my life, Heidi's, the people I met. On Ibiza. Where after not long, if longer than the week I had thought to stay, I had a run-in with the local law.

Heidi went home, I went to jail. I did not expect to hear from her again. Not after I had sobered up and realised the treatment I had meted out.

It was September, handcuffed in Majorca, where they have a court and a prison proper, that they let me out for a run to the airport and flight to London.

Deported.

London. My heart was sore on the run to town. I had not, as might be supposed, been on the wagon during my time in jail. I was not drunk as I'd liked, but hardly on the wagon. You can, or could at that time in Spanish jails, get drink—if you had money you could get drink.

But with that behind me I got the Glasgow train. Again. I was getting fed up with London, Euston and the Glasgow train. I was getting fed up with a whole lot of things after my time in jail, and was seriously worried about my drinking.

Again.

I was worried about my drinking but drinking.

The first drink they hammered into you at AA.

I saw the wisdom.

It is a hard wisdom not to see unless you don't want to see it.

I didn't, not even then after a summer in jail—no, I still wanted to drink. I wished not to get drunk, go to jail again, but I still wanted to drink.

Still I cut it down, I had no money and had to cut it down, but when I could I drank, got as drunk as I had ever been. My life, for again I had nothing, was back to navvying and digging roads, seemed a shambles with no way out, or only one. For I still thought money, my lack of it, was my main problem. I recognised booze, but money, which to get I swung a pick to spend in pubs, seemed so much more important. Christmas approached, a time of good cheer.

So I took a chance and again—as so many times—I had a stake and I quit on work.

Christmas passed, in January or February the telephone rang.

My mother answered: 'It's for you.'

'Hullo,' I said.

'It's me, Heidi.'

I was very surprised but hid it well: 'How are you?'

'A *mother*,' she said.

'Indeed. When?'

'Two days ago.'

'I'm sorry,' I said.

'I wanted the baby.'

'I meant about Spain.'

'We could forget Spain.'

I had after my penance, months in jail and hustle here in Glasgow, forgotten her. I had so short a memory when I chose. 'Is it a boy or a girl?'

'A girl.'

'She's well?'

'We're both well.'

I didn't know what to say at this, out of the blue.

'I thought,' she said, 'that you should know.'

'Of course.'

'It's a surprise?'

'You can say that again, it's a surprise.' But I felt nothing, neither elated nor deflated. Nothing. And sober. I was off drink, after New Year and a bout through January I was off booze, for as ever I could quit, stop with not even a shandy, for a week or a month, but I could not stay stopped. I was to take a lot more punishment, the very gates of hell, no understatement the gates of hell, before I—well, one day at a time, that I *am* sober now.

'I mean,' she said, 'you had to know.'

'Sure.' It was like talking to a stranger, the woman who had had my baby.

'You could come out.'

'I'd like to come out.'

'She looks like you.'

'A girl, she looks like me?'

'Her eyes,' Heidi said.

'Then I must come out.'

We spoke. About the baby, her, me, the man I was and no shit as before I told her the truth, that I had no money, no nothing.

'It doesn't matter.'

'No?'

'I'll send you money.'

'I've money enough to come to Germany.'

'You will come.'

'I'll come.'

'Promise?'

'I promise.'

But I got drunk instead, the kid got christened. Heidi telephoned and I still was drinking.

And I wanted to go to Germany.

My mother and my sister, they urged me to go. A couple of times I had my suitcase packed and almost went, and would have gone if not, in the midst of that bout, by then March, I *saw* things.

It was morning. I was sitting at the fire, smoking with a

glass of wine, when a grizzly bear gave me a wink. I was a little dismayed, a little alarmed, but I almost jumped when a tiger appeared.

Sitting in my chair. Drinking. I had a couple of stiff jolts. I knew in the sane part of my head that there was nothing there, no animals. Yet I saw and heard—I even smelled them.

I was alone, or just me and the bear and the tiger, a big Bengal, that in a snarl and a leap attacked the bear, a fight to the death. I knew it was a fight to the death and hoped for the bear, its wink was friendly so that I might reason with it, to win.

The roars, the blood, those beasts, were awful.

I remember it all.

Some six monkeys, prancing bastards, the boss was a chimp who wore a hat with a feather, he hopped up on my knee and he had a swig of my wine.

'Good stuff,' he professed, and I patted his head, but he said snappily, 'Mind the fucking feather.'

I had glimpses of tall giraffes, striped zebras and two billy goats who held a butting contest.

A whole zoo was by then in my house: grunting pigs, flamboyant peacocks, a couple of doves, while the monkey who wore the feather, the chimp on my knee, bared his teeth and bit my nose.

I felt the pain.

I tried to hit him and punched the wall.

The bastard then hopped on the head of the bear, who after his fight with the tiger was in a pretty bad way, but this was a very safe place for the chimp to be.

All of this while the billy goats still battered heads. I heard the cracks. Big goats kicked their hoofs and snorted like bulls.

I watched in amazement. Where the fuck had they all come from?

How many years drinking?

So real.

It ended, the bedlam. I could take no more, I went under the table.

It was where my mother found me, under the table.

Night.

I had a terrible hangover, but the creatures were all gone, and of course, something like sane again, I did not say anything about my visitors.

Indeed I thought I might have dreamt it.

I examined my nose, there was no bite, I thought to have dreamt it, only why when I opened my eyes was I under the table?

No, those things were the conjure of my addled mind, they were real all right, the chimp with the feather had bitten my nose (my fist was swollen from my punch at the wall), to have me under the table.

Yet I washed and shaved, went out that night, if in the pub drinking beer, I was subdued. It was in my mind, the attack, demon creatures, had it happened outside, in the open, I might well be in the madhouse.

I sat alone in the pub, and it was nothing unusual that I sat, drank alone in pubs.

It would be wrong though if I implied that I sat, a pariah. I knew lots of guys, but usually I preferred to sit alone, and they for their part hardly forced their company.

But that night after my visions of the morning, I was more alone and more withdrawn.

Physically I was tough. I could recover from a bender in two or three days, but *mentally*—no man should hide beneath a table.

I drank just beer, no wine, the thing about my jungle juice, jungle scene, the bear and the tiger, the chimp with the feather, butting billy-goats, fluttering doves, was it had been so *real*.

My nose still hurt it had been so real.

I determined to eat while I was drinking. I had to force-feed myself, but I determined to eat. It was after no food, my vision, all the reason that I could come up with. Or all I wanted to come up with.

I had been drinking then, on that bender, for about a month.

Previously during my drinking and the trouble I was in, I worried about imprisonment, a duel with the law, now for worse, I worried about mental wards.

There was no doubt in my mind that after the things I had seen and my reaction, if I had been in a public place I would have been committed to a mental ward.

Yet now just hours after, things showed normal and with some logic I was able to think.

I drank a few beers, wandered to a few pubs, had a look at the moon—I was so desperate it would have suited me to see a full moon, some excuse.

Night.

Bed.

I had come to dread it.

Bed.

Night.

That night.

There were shadowy creatures as I tossed in bed.

I wished, I cursed myself, for Nembutal.

Just two of those yellow capsules would do the trick.

My heart beat, hammered. I fancied, in the heart of the city, to hear an owl.

And I had not been drinking heavily, compared to what I drank I had not been drinking heavily.

I was too scared of a return to the jungle scene, to drink too heavily.

Sober.

The owl appeared.

In the dark.

One eye luminous.

Vivid.

Wild.

Just one eye, a wink to me—who knew it was a phantom.

In the dark.

I switched on the light.

The owl stayed, still hung, sat in the void, but with a duller eye.

I rested, could you call it that, with an owl for company, the light burning the whole night through.

Next day, after such a night, that fucking owl, I presented myself to the doctor.

I complained, no lie, of insomnia and jangled nerves.

He knew about my drinking and was a bit reluctant about the Nembutal, he warned me of booze and Nembutal, a fatal combination.

I could have told him.

But after that thing, the owl, the night and day, the jungle scene I had endured, I was determined if not to stop, to cut back on booze, and rather than risk all that again, I had to begin, for the first few days, to lean on drugs.

I got tranquillisers, vitamin tablets, the Nembutal, that and a sickness certificate for nervous debility, to assist me in my effort.

It was all the doctor could do, or if I had told him the truth of my hallucinations, refer me to a hospital, where I guess that same treatment would have been about all that they could do.

Remember I had been to Alcoholics Anonymous.

I began on a triple dose of the tranquillisers.

It was a dreadful hangover, phantom bite, still hurting nose.

I had a couple of pints. The day was raw and cold. I felt a bit more secure on the Nembutal, a sure knowledge of a sleep with no visions, and could only wonder I had survived the day and night, the owl, wild beasts, and no one knowing. There was some pride in that, or so I thought, for it was only women who hid under fucking tables.

The day passed.

I took the vitamin tablets, the tranquillisers and, at night after a couple of Nembutal, I retired early.

It felt in the morning like the first decent sleep I had had in months.

It was the first time truly, alive and well, eating again and sane, that I was glad to be sober.

I was still on the wagon in May when I went to the town on the Rhine, for a visit to my baby daughter.

I remember she gripped my finger with both her hands, and would not let go.

I was astonished at her perfection, miniature. The weight, heat of her, blonde, big blue eyes, and how scared I was, holding her, that she might fall.

Here, she, that baby, was something mine. So helpless, snug and trusting it almost broke my heart. And if coming I had wished for a boy, I did not care that she was a daughter.

But also Heidi's daughter and Heidi was a fierce, protective mother.

We became lovers again in the town on the Rhine, a medieval town, cobbled, with towers and spires and taverns that sold wine and strong cool beer. You could get drunk on the beer, as I did drinking with Heidi's father, a man who had fought at Stalingrad, had been captured and spent time in Russia.

In Germany.

Where, for a time with Heidi and a baby I adored, I was happy.

But I drank, got drunk. I could not help when drinking

getting drunk. And drunk I got in fights. Stupid, crazy fights.

Heidi's father, a man who had fought at Stalingrad, who knew men, who, when I was in jail had to bail me out, warned—and I do not blame him—his daughter against marriage to me.

I called him a Nazi bastard.

We fought.

It was the end of the line, that time in Germany.

I miss a lot. I miss the old man, a guy I liked and respected, his offer of a house and job. I who had nothing. I miss that Heidi, if not true love it was not far short, as a wife I could have done much worse. I miss the baby, how I missed, miss even now, the baby. But I could not stop drinking. It was killing, ruining me as a man but I could not stop drinking. Once begun I could not stop. The stuff was breaking my balls, bursting my head, and yet I could not stop it.

The first drink.

But I could not get the message, would not accept that after the first drink I became powerless over booze.

I was not an alcoholic.

I went, nevertheless, on my return from Germany, back to Alcoholics Anonymous. But again they failed, or I failed. The thing was just too simple, or I was too simple, but the message they preached I could not get.

It was a dreadful time.

A fight to survive.

Nights on Nembutal, I was stuffed at night on Nembutal, and not prescribed, but I needed the dope to get some sleep, to stop me screaming. And physically, with little food, near starvation, I was failing. The meat on my arms and thighs, my chest, was falling away. This summer, in July or August I remember a plague of boils on my return from Germany. People like my mother thought me broken-hearted, which I was—by Christ I was, and if only in McNeil Street, in the

Pig and Whistle, I could have seen this. Hooked as bad as a
junkie, totally lost, I would have shunned the stuff for a
devil's gift.

Yet stubborn with stupid pride I could not admit that
booze had me beat.

In the pit I could not admit booze had me beat.

It was the worst till then, times had been so bad I thought
they could get no worse, but I was wrong.

I was rescued from that bout, that time of despair by a
stay in a monastery. I was a candidate for a hospital bed but
not wanting that—dear fuck, no—I ended up in the monastery where I stayed till December.

But this was no cure, if at the time it might have saved
my life and I was back drinking by Christmas and drunk by
New Year.

Still, that stay in the monastery was good for me. A bit of
peace and quiet. I studied theology. But the more I read, the
less I knew. There was, for what it's worth, nothing under-
hand, no booze or drugs or illicit sex in that monastery, a
place of prayer, pure and simple.

I had talks with the monks about theology, my life and
theirs but it was something like my flirt with AA. I either
did not want it or I could not get it.

I plundered the library of holy works, the lives of the
saints, but I could not find God.

So I tired of saintly reading, the only reading, and like
I was flung back on myself, I began again to write short
stories. A little room, more cell than room, a clear head,
no booze or drugs, I took no booze and I required no
drugs. I wrote stories about my childhood, fictioned fact,
with no thought of plot, and one or two of those stories,
my work in the monastery, they came out good enough to
be published, to win me a travel fellowship the following
summer.

I got help and encouragement from one particular monk,
a writer himself, a wonderful man but a worthless writer.

His stuff was junk. Honesty compels me to say that his stuff was junk. And for my own writing this was no bad thing, as in reading his stories, mine came out better than good.

The time passed.

I was the sole guest in that place—there had been quite a hassle to get me in—and I grew fit and strong and mentally sharp. The first time for a long time I thought to be gaining strength. Long walks, wholesome food, good company—the monks were surprisingly good company—but I have to stick to the issue. Booze. And no booze in the monastery, I must move on back to Glasgow to my mother's house, where as there was nowhere else I returned.

I was a bit embarrassed as people knew where I'd been, but I was drinking again—it seems incredible, where booze had taken me, but drinking again on my first day out—I made out to be cured.

Indeed I got a job as a night guard for a construction company. In Shettleston, Glasgow, where after two bottles of wine I got arrested. I was about two weeks out of the monastery. Cured? I was arrested for being drunk and disorderly and lost the job—I had worked, been employed for six hours at most. This after my treatment, long months in the monastery, the prayers of the monks, was a terrible blow. I had had such hopes for a decent life, trying to become a writer, that I had taken the job to be alone at nights, my try to become a writer.

Dashed.

A visit to a pub, The Marquis, and two bottles of wine.

I had been in worse trouble, much worse, but this after such hopes and months on the wagon—if only in the monastery those months on the wagon—it seemed the end. I was so miserable. In jail. Morning. Sobering up. I pleaded not guilty. I think, bleary-eyed, still reeking of wine, I astonished the court by my plea of not guilty. But they did not know my head, the shame I felt: I just could not admit to being drunk.

I walked out of the court—they had fixed a date for my trial—and into a pub. The Tartan Bar. I sat in the lounge. Empty. I was, at eleven o'clock, first customer of the day. Drinking. Sacked. I knew I was sacked after my first night in jail and as I had no more to lose, I got drunk as I'd been. Another black-out, I awoke in London.

Morning.

Yet I had been home, for I was dressed in a winter coat and with a travelling bag I arrived in Euston Station.

The place was the same, the people, the liquor store in Euston Road, where I bought some whisky.

Not three weeks out of the monastery. Sitting in that station, drinking whisky from the bottle.

And again, arriving at that station, all the times I had come, drinking, a loneliness I could not fathom. Even drunk, the loneliness, and I thought about going home—until the pubs opened I thought to go home.

I was ashamed to be again in London but even more ashamed of my night in jail and I was all mixed-up and drunk and drinking in the London pubs that as a boy I had thought so jolly, so full of cheer, but were the loneliest dives.

At first.

Off the train.

The whisky and first couple of pints.

Then, as ever in such places my mood swung. It was Christmastime, or almost, London bright with Christmas trees, fairy lights, and I thought to have a last, a *final* binge—what the fuck, this feeling blue. I had suffered enough, months in a monastery, I was due a drink.

Insanity?

I thought not to think about what had me in the monastery.

I quaffed the beer with more relish then. My final drink. A session for I thought three or four days—at most three or four days before I kicked the traces, was done with the stuff forever.

Another man, he might have pulled it off, a three or four day drunk to be free, sober ever after.

Even me at that late date, I almost turned the trick.

So it can be done, a considered last bout.

But my three or four day drinking went on for a week and had me in hospital.

That was another added blow.

I would have preferred jail.

Much rathered jail, for after the monastery and all the months of good food, vitamins by the fistful, exercise, I thought to be in good shape, fit for longer than one week's drinking.

I had booked into a hotel, a decent place, bed and breakfast and evening meal (though I ate nothing) and a late night bar, for it being my last drink I saw no reason to scrimp.

I even phoned home the good news to my mother, about my last drink.

I think in London those people I met, the hotel staff, barmen, I must have bored them stiff about my last drink.

But, as said I said, I almost pulled it off.

After two fights, real wild-west stuff, I awoke in the hospital. I remember the fights, they happened during my first two days, but I remember nothing about how I went to hospital.

First I awoke, naked, in bed, in a white sheet, I thought I was in the morgue. I jumped up stark naked, a bound right out of that bed, thinking it a terrible mistake.

The room had a high round window and by day I saw the light, pale winter sun, shine through the window. I looked around for other stiffs, but was alone in the room. Quiet. Hushed. A silence that hurt. And cold, by fuck it was cold, or I was cold, I looked for my clothes. Nowhere. Nothing. Not a stitch. I found the door and it was locked. I was still sure, white sheet to my chin, alone in the room, that I was in the morgue. In London. At least I knew I was in London.

I began to hammer on the door.

Two nurses came, young girls, pretty, one in blue. They rustled. Smiled. I demanded to know where I was and why.

'The doctor is coming.'

'Get me my clothes.'

'When you see the doctor.'

'I don't want to see no fucking doctor.'

'He wants to see you.'

I sat on the edge of the bed. They stood. Smiling. One was Irish. The sun from the round window, still filtered in. I pulled over the sheet for a bit of modesty.

Not a month out of the monastery.

The doctor came.

A white-haired man, but not old, about forty, best as I could figure, in my condition, just wanting out and away from this place, he looked about forty.

'Mr Thorn?'

'That's me.'

'How do you feel?'

'How would you feel?'

The nurses, behind him, out of his sight, giggled. I felt a fool in this place in front of those girls, naked—and I worried and hoped that my drawers were clean. I had suffered enough humiliation.

'I'm asking you,' the doctor said.

'Okay. I feel okay.'

'You want to know what happened?'

'I only want out of here.'

'I think you should stay a couple of days—you know, observation.'

'No.'

'You're sure?'

'Definite.'

'I think you should stay.'

'Just get me my clothes.'

'I want to help you.'

'Doctor, I just had a drink.'

'You had more than that, I think—*just* a drink.'

'Look, I'm sorry—if I caused any trouble I'm sorry.'

'Do you always awake in hospital when you take a drink?'

'No. Of course I don't.'

'Then,' he said, 'all the more reason that you should stay.'

'I'm not staying.'

He shrugged. 'I can't make you stay.'

'Then please get me my clothes.'

'You don't want to know what happened?'

'I just want my clothes.'

He signalled to one of the nurses.

'I'm sorry,' I said, repeated.

'You're an alcoholic?'

'No.' I felt a bit better with the nurse away to get my clothes. 'I told you I just take a drink.'

'You don't want help?' he asked.

'I don't need help.'

He asked me for a urine sample.

'Now?'

'It's as good a time as any.'

The remaining nurse held me a jar.

I padded, still buck, behind a screen.

My head cracked.

The nurse came with my clothes.

I signed a paper.

The doctor gave me a couple of jags in the hip before I dressed—painful shots whatever they were.

'You won't stay?'

'No.'

The man was trying to help me.

'Then,' he said, 'the best of luck.'

I dressed.

Went.

The nurse showed me the way.

Out of the hospital and out to the streets of Glasgow.

I got a taxi home and went directly to bed with two Nembutal. Yellow submarines? It was me who was sinking. Fast. This could not go on. I had little idea where I had been, what hotel in London, the day or date of my coming home.

In bed waiting for sleep, for the Nembutal to work, the drop into blackness, surcease to my raging head.

I did not know, was not sure, if Christmas was past or was to come.

And I was wishing now that I had asked the doctor how come I was in hospital?

But my mind was such that I was not even sure about the hospital.

This bed that I lay in, I thought it was home.

That was all, just thought, I was sure about nothing.

I smoked, a bad habit with Nembutal, even with no booze, to smoke in bed. I felt thirsty, in need of a piss, but could not be bothered to rise for a drink or a piss.

I thought I would have a couple more Nembutal for sleep, there were some shapes in the dark, it seemed a long time coming, but could not be bothered either with that effort.

I lay and deep-breathed on my back and the rain outside, I heard it splutter, was the last recall of that dreadful night.

Morning.

Bright.

Cold.

I was tempted to take more Nembutal for a merciful sleep, but I was full of curiosity about yesterday, for I was still not sure about yesterday in the hospital, my trip to London and back.

The whole thing dawned a nightmare.

I hoped that it was a nightmare.

But there was some hurt in my hip, a stiffness, and I looked and saw the needle marks, flesh purple-blue, a reddish hue, and that was no dream. My head ached so that

I could barely lift it, as if it weighed like a lump of lead, and it was a torture to get out of bed.

I dressed in my trousers and shirt. I had slept in my drawers.

I went through to the kitchen where my mother was and opened a can of beer.

The fire was lit, burning bright, and outside the rooftops, the streets, were washed with rain.

I drank my beer.

'Maybe if I bought a dog.'

'If you want a dog.'

I had not till then even thought of a dog.

She sat, I sat. There was some whisky, stuff I had bought for Christmas—it was still to come, Christmas and the New Year.

I poured a glass. Drank. I had no shakes, and was glad of that. With the whisky I drank I suffered no poke. But a dead morning, I had no heart, no spirit either.

'I don't know,' I said, 'I feel so lonely.'

It was the first time I had told anyone about my loneliness.

'You don't need tae be lonely.'

I knew what she meant.

Germany.

'She's phoned, you know.'

'Heidi?'

'While you were in the monastery.'

'You didn't say I was in the monastery?'

'No,' my mother said, 'I never told.'

Pride.

I still had pride.

The morning, the rain, the day grey as my mood. 'My life,' I said, 'it's one fucking mess.'

'It's only you kin do something about it.'

'I just don't seem to know no more.'

We sat. I drank. Smoked. And again as ever, if slowly, I recovered some spirit, as fight returned to my beaten head, and I was ashamed that I had spoken so of my loneliness, that before my mother I was a little boy again.

The bastard was, it was worse than that: I was a missing man.

My mother was not five foot tall.

She made me food that I struggled to eat; I threw it in the fire. The day dragged. Long. I tried to read, but I could not read, concentrate.

We had in the window a Christmas tree, lit up, that when darkness fell, glowed homely and warm in the winter night.

I stood by the window, it was a habit; in many rooms I had stood by many windows.

The telephone rang and I knew it was Heidi.

How?

I don't know how.

My mother was out.

I let the phone ring.

Fuck her, Heidi, I was a different man now—let her write, send a letter. I had had enough of her last phone calls.

Heartache. It was all she brought me. Her last phone calls had near broke my heart. For me to rot in a monastery. I blamed Heidi for the monastery.

Standing by the window. Drinking. Not drunk, not sober, a carefree mood not giving a damn.

The hospital, yesterday, and the days preceding, the London nights, had a dream-like quality.

There was no use. Those days were gone, lost, as if they never had been, to worry about them.

Both of my hands, my fists, were swollen, mementoes of my fights.

London.

I hoped never to see that city again.

Or police, those bastards who had stolen my job, my night as a guard arrested as a drunk. I remembered still the shame of that.

Anger.

Rage and impotence. Those cops, it swelled in me. My try for an honest life, my efforts to become a writer.

It would be true that with the hate I felt, as a Samson in chains, I could have killed each cop I saw.

There was nothing dream-like about my night in jail, the loss of my job.

I tossed back the whisky, by the window. A rage so great that I could have smashed the window, the Christmas tree.

So small, a thing, a night in jail. After the trouble I'd known, it amazes me yet the rage that I felt. But it amazes me too that that I had not years before, but especially then after full months in a monastery, stopped drinking.

I went for a shower, a change, for I was smelling myself and feeling funky.

It would then have been about six o'clock, some two or three days till Christmas.

My body remained hard and muscled, even if now the hair on my chest was turning silver. It was the first time in that shower, the hair on my chest, that I had noticed. I shaved. A week's growth, beard of sorts, and in my face, my eyes, I saw my father.

Dead.

Bones.

I remembered the day they buried him, not caring really, as I was feeling more free, a boy in a graveyard in lashing rain.

Yet that was the day my troubles started.

Had I known what troubles I would have wept, cried my eyes out in that graveyard. His face was my face, at the eyes, and I had not thought to look like my father. I had till then forgotten, or thought to have forgotten how he had looked. Yet a glimpse, a blink, for as he came and he went I saw him in the mirror.

Smiling at the mirror I looked at my teeth, a couple of bad ones, the scars round my eyes, about sixty stitches patched my eyes, but I was looking younger, a whole lot younger than I was.

I felt older. Sometimes in the morning I felt all of ninety years old.

Dressing.

I felt much better washed and shaved, changed.

If I had quit on booze in the monastery I could quit it in the city. But the time, season of the year was wrong. I thought I would quit afterwards, in January.

A new year.

New me.

It was my resolve.

And as I said, I almost did it.

Almost.

The story of my life, the long saga, my drinking.

Drinking while planning to stop.

But I was determined, even though I had liked the monastery and the monks, there would be no further visit.

A logical day. Night. Rested. Washed. Shaved. About a bottle of whisky but I was nothing drunk. Watching television, catching up on the news after a week of no news, reading letters.

The telephone rang, I answered—gave my number.

'Michael', she said.

'Speaking.'

'It's me, Heidi.'

'I know.'

'How are you?'

'I'm fine—how are you.'

'I'm pregnant,' she said, a pause, 'again.'

'You must be a long time pregnant.'

'I couldn't reach you before.'

'No,' I said, ' I know.'

'You were in jail?'

'No, I wasn't in jail—I was in jail last week, but only for a night.'

'Drunk?'

'Sure.'

'But I've been trying,' she said, 'for months to reach you.'

'You must be a glutton for punishment if you have been trying for months to reach me.'

'It's your child.'

'I know.'

'Michael, you could do better.'

'I intend to try to do better.'

'We could,' she said, 'work it out. I know we could work it out.'

'The Beatles used to sing that, remember *We Can Work it Out*?'

'I love you.'

'Then you must be crazy, loving me.'

'I don't care if I'm crazy.'

We spoke awhile, I felt glad and sad. Proud that she loved me, but I would not now, with a new baby, chance my heart again.

She would phone back she said, and I went to bed and thought about her, how we had met in Sydney and London, and two babies soon, and I wondered could we make it, build something good from out of chaos. I hoped for a boy, with all my heart I hoped for a boy. I loved the girl, but hoped this time for a baby boy.

Christmas I tried to behave, get not too drunk, and succeeded in part to get blasted at New Year.

I drank and stayed drunk from Hogmanay till 6 January, when, against all the expectations of the people who knew me, I quit.

Not a lick after January 6th. I was wise about the first drink and the compulsion after, and for the first few days I lived on drugs. The Nembutal and tranquillisers. But after a week off the booze I quit the medicine. The sad truth was after one drug, alcohol, I had in those first few days to find a substitute. It was the easy way, perhaps short of hospital, the only way.

But I came off booze in early January, and for a long time—for me a very long time—till autumn, late September, I was on the wagon.

I got a job as a school janitor. I would have taken any job to get me out, out of myself, my melancholia, and it just happened that I got a job as a relief school janitor.

Thinking to get my house in order. I changed my plea, pleaded guilty to the drunken charge. By letter. And got fined ten pounds, also by letter.

That was March, I think, with two children by now, with a baby boy, and the job of school janitor but looking for better. It was usual that, sober, I was looking for better, for more.

But after a few months of hard-won freedom, and it was hard-won and no mistake, even with the drugs I was not unhappy in the job as school janitor.

Heidi phoned and I wrote to her often.

I doted on the kids even at a distance, and Heidi's father, some surprise, he offered me a job again.

His job was much better paying, about five times more than at my work in schools, but I was sober in my work in schools. And not wanting to get drunk, to chance at this stage my sobriety, I declined. The horror of my past was still too recent.

I fought for sobriety. Without it I had nothing. I acted nonchalant, like it was easy, and maybe that was because I dreaded to drink.

At night sometimes during the first few weeks I would awake in the early hours with sheer terror at the thought that I had drunk.

The first drink.

I clung on for months, a bulldog hold. Sweeping school playgrounds. The winter went on to spring and I clung to the memory of my last drink, the first drink.

But by summertime the memory had faded. Like an old photograph. A duller pain. And I had some thought again that I could drink, take a couple and leave it at that.

I was doomed by that thinking, long before I actually drank, for nothing was more sure than that I would drink.

In May or June I won a travel award—a reward for the stories I had written in the monastery. And wanting to write, but with no time to write, not till then in my job as a janitor.

I worked as a janitor for long hours, night school, and I had written nothing since the monastery.

But my win was a boost, and I thought I might try again, a novel—I had in my head the seed of the book, the fiction of me at sixteen years-old adrift in London.

I was sure that my novel, a tale of a boy-bandit, would be a winner all the way—if I could write it.

I figured the work for a short novel was a three-month stint—no more than that. With short stories of three or four thousand words I could write one a day or in two days at most. So a novel, a short one, if a different form, I thought three months would be plenty, with time to spare.

I quit the schools and with no booze had enough money with the travel award and with what I had saved, I began on the work in July.

Man-bandit, my tale of a boy-bandit. At the end of a month of writing it worked out to be longer and nothing like I had thought.

That was after a month.

August.

September I got stuck, the thing just would not work, yield an inch, my tale of a boy-bandit—I sat sore-arsed for hours and it would not work, give an inch.

It would be true, if there is anything that drives a man to drink that book drove me, who for some time had thought to drink.

This was in 1975, my first real effort to write. The other

stuff was just in absent moments. But I was stuck on it then in September. Long months on the wagon, I went to Germany. Sober. I went by train and boat, and through London again and Paris, but made it to Germany, to the town on the Rhine without a drink.

It was a beautiful time with the children. I bounced my daughter, cuddled my son, had him on my chest, the beat of my heart, fall fast asleep.

But I wanted drink. All the time in the three weeks I was there, I wanted drink. I made love with Heidi and I could almost taste the booze. I walked around the town, cobbled streets, autumn air, and had a beautiful woman, beautiful children, all a man could wish for, yet I wanted drink.

It was the overriding passion.

And I could not understand it. I had been off the stuff for fucking months. But a terrible craving and it ruined that time in Germany in the town on the Rhine. I did not drink, with a mighty effort I did not drink, but it ruined the time.

Marking time, in Paris or London, to get drunk.

I thought not now a drink but drunk.

It was why in Germany I did not drink.

But I was startled a bit by booze, by my awful obsession, with no reason to drink or get drunk, rather the opposite, every reason to stay sober.

There was something wrong, even alcoholic, and after so long with no first drink, this compulsion.

Something wrong?

My thinking was wrong from the first. In January when I had stopped, for rather than quit I had only abstained.

And during the weeks to months of winter to summer to autumn, the longer I was sober the more the nag was there that I could drink.

Baffling.

Insidious.

Cunning.

Words I had heard at my AA meetings.

It was all of them and more—the craving I had in Germany.

An almost physical torture as I passed by bars and smelled the stuff. I even once, as though sucked in like a bit of filing to a magnet, stood at a bar and ordered a drink. Paid for it but, some sanity, a smiling sigh—I remember smiling—I walked out again and walked for miles, far out of the town and up to the hills. Grassy slopes where like some suffering Christ I sat for hours with a view over the Rhine, the town, and why the fuck this dirty affliction, weird condition, that I could not trust myself to drink?

I wanted the kids and Heidi. If only to get the kids I wanted Heidi, and again through my good behaviour, a date was fixed for our wedding.

I did not, it amazes me still, but I did not drink immediately after I left Germany. I spent a night in Paris and I did not drink. I ached for a drink but did not drink, and I think had I gone just another few days, a week at most, the compulsion would have gone.

What might have been—it could have you scurry back to the bottle to think about what might have been. I got drunk on duty-free booze on the boat to Dover. Drunk and with a huge carry-out, I had about twenty bottles, litres of whisky, as a carry-out. The customs waved me through. A train to London. I had in London with the weight of my cargo, at Waterloo Station—an apt name—to get assistance with a taxi to Euston.

I was a different man from the man who had come, when I arrived in Euston Station. Drinking. Drunk. Waiting for my train. Strange, weird thoughts, that I would be better off without the children, that Heidi had tricked me somehow.

Mad.

I was more than mad.

Twenty bottles of whisky, that stuff made me mad.

This was the first day's drinking.

As the days went on I would get madder. But I made it

home from Euston to Glasgow Central, and with no delay, if only because of the whisky I made it home with no delay—or delay only in Glasgow where I stopped the taxi to buy some beer to hasten me on. *Delirium tremens*, the weirdest encounter of all my life.

Drink. If I had drunk before, it was like kindergarden, and supposedly cured; after long sober months I drank for three weeks on the fiercest non-stop bout that for a normal man might have lasted a year.

Heidi phoned and I told her in no uncertain terms what I did *not* think of her.

Drinking.

Not eating.

Not sleeping.

Violent.

I punched and burst up my hands, hooked doors off hinges—Heidi phoned and I told her again what I did not think, and, my tirade done, I wrecked the phone. The bastard, that bout, I wrecked more than just the phone. All this, a madman raging, while my mother looked on: my mother who did not drink and who must have wondered where all this would end.

But powerless.

She as I was powerless.

The first drink.

I now could not stop.

If before in Germany on the boat to Dover I had a choice, I had no choice now.

I had pals—I still had a few—who would visit me and bring in drink, for I seldom went out, and the twenty bottles went long before the bout was over.

Again I grew a beard.

My mother begged and pleaded with me to stop drinking. She even had the priest visit, but he came and went, and on his advice my mother went too. I did not even notice.

This would have been the third week's drinking when I

was more occupied with gods than mortals.

I had on booze an acid trip.

There was little difference between the LSD I took on the trip to Afghanistan, trying to reach Katmandu, those things I saw and remember yet, if colours that I can't describe, and that orgy on booze.

They began well.

Angels.

St Peter blew his horn.

I sat in a storm of angels, beating wings. Thirsty birds who after a while, when I was not looking, began to steal my booze.

That was the beginning, robbing angels, birds I had mistaken from heaven, imps from hell, beatific smiles to werewolf fangs, of the nightmare time.

Of course, on the booze I was going mad. Some spark in my head told me so, that the things I saw were not there. Even as they snapped, bloody fangs, fetid breath an inch from my nose, I knew that they were not there. But there or not, apparitions—what is an apparition?—they were awful real to me.

I remember a pal who was there, true flesh and blood and my amazement; the imps, that he did not see them.

The whole thing was a panorama. The most vivid light. And there is more, I am sure, than what you see and what exists and it might be there is a lot of talent in a madhouse.

Whatever, the imps above with beating wings, they shat on me. Giant turds burst on my head to drip down my face, and I saw the shit on my hands, *smelt* it with my nose, and I was not pleased at this treatment.

So attacked.

Indeed I did. And killed a few. Cut off their heads with a cutlass blade, until the boss imp—I thought him worried—called a truce: 'Enough.'

I sat down, he sat down: 'Get rid of your men,' I told him. The imps, half of them dead, the others ruffled and dishevelled; licking their wounds, wings, sat a sorry crew.

I felt mighty pleased with the carnage and sat with my cutlass.

'You have killed a good half of us.'

The cutlass wept, ran red with blood.

'And for that,' he said, 'you deserve a treat.'

I was ready for anything, that foxy bastard. His one eye, round, red, above his beak of yellow, which given his wings and a man's torso, skinny legs in tight bright pants, I thought not at all unusual.

I fenced with the cutlass (I'd fancy the poker) and demanded my treat, saying, 'It had better be good'.

'Have no fear.'

I looked round the house at the dead imps, broken wings, a scatter of one-eyed heads, and proud, bursting with pride told him, 'It's you should worry.'

'We will parry.'

'Fuck parry.' I felt after the carnage, dead imps, to have the upper hand. 'I want my treat.'

'Patience.'

'I've shown enough patience.'

He smoked a long cigarette in an ivory holder, sat cross-legged—skinny, spider-legged in the tight bright pants—and deep in thought.

'My treat, you bastard.'

'I'm thinking.'

'You take a long time to think.'

'What would you want?'

'A bag of gold.'

'That's not enough.'

'Two bags of gold.'

He shook his head, one sparkling eye, two bags of gold still not enough.

I thought, I remember, mad as I was I remember thinking of capturing him, putting him in a bottle—I don't know how at the size of him as big as me, but casting around for an empty bottle I looked again and he was gone, replaced in the chair by the most luscious blonde.

Just me and her. Alone. All the imps, even the dead imps well gone.

My treat.

She was like lady Godiva, her hair hid her tits. Such a tease—if on a chair and not a horse.

Smiling.

Good teeth.

Blue eyes.

I remember her teeth, and two blue eyes, no wings, but the tumbling hair hid her charms.

I still held the cutlass poker. 'We will dance.'

'No.'

'Why not?'

'Let's talk awhile.'

'Fuck talk. I'm fed up talking.'

'Get,' she said, 'to know each other.' She sat, legs curled under her, a glimpse of nipple but nothing more. 'It would be better if we got to know each other.'

But I was not to be denied which was a mistake, for I went to yank her up, and she lashed me with her tail. Wet. Salt. A tang of the sea.

I sat down again.

'I'm sorry,' she said.

'You should have told me.'

'It's not easy,' she said, 'a girl with a tail.'

'It's a lovely tail.' And truly it was. This was a mermaid, and not really a tail, rather an appendage thick and shiny and winking colour, a flipper base. And now with her hair flung back over her shoulders, the most exotic, erotic picture—if I did wonder about such a woman, how to *make* it.

But not for long, for as sudden as she had come she went and the imp returned.

'That was my treat?'

'You're jesting,' he said, 'I've a lot better for a man like you.'

'Yes?'

'We're pals,' he said.

'Fetch her back.'

'After.'

'Now.'

'You know who I am?'

'No.'

'Take a look.'

I did, at his one red eye which glowed, grew bigger, and I saw, *heard* things in it, all the horrors of the ages, shrieks and screams and villainous laughter, cannibal feasts, glutton eaters, bloody babies, tremendous battles. I think Joan of Arc, the siege of Troy, the death at the stake of Joan of Arc—but a hundred deaths—and hers was *mild*—before this awful show ended, the eye contracted and I sat with the *Devil*. Such a terrible sight that I fled the house.

It was daytime.

Bright.

Cold.

I fled barefoot bare-chested in a run to the priest, who, a credit to him, listened to my ravings—though I vowed him to silence as I was not so mad as to risk the madhouse—and I calmed a bit as he drove me home.

This was fact, I have enquired.

I ended up at the end of that bout back in the monastery. Another fact. Sad. And feeling I had lost everything, I knew I had lost Heidi. In the monastery, silent time, old stone walls, long table where we ate. Escape? No. I was just out of temptation. Cured? I would never be cured, a man who could drink much more than most yet who could not drink at all. There was irony. Somewhere. But hardly a smile in me. I was back again in my old room on a diet of pills, vitamins and Nembutal, trying hard to return as a man.

That was the second week, for despite all the pills, vitamins and tranquillisers, the Nembutal, during the first week I had the shakes, sweats, and riding over the drugs, the feeling that it was all over. Past. No appetite for food *or* life, as though death would be a mercy.

My conundrum, if I shrugged at life I still fought to live, and, certainly, I never thought of suicide.

That was the first week when with only a small recall of coming here, I was at my lowest.

But in the second week I was bouncing back. Eating. I started to eat and I started to heal. It was always the same with drinking. After heavy sessions as I started to eat I began to recover. Physically. But mentally it was hard to accept (though I did my best to hide it) that I was back in the monastery.

The monks—well I liked the monks and think that they liked me.

There was another drunkard this time in the monastery, a retired sea captain, who like me had had a flirt with AA and was for a second time in the monastery.

I could tell that man's story, from long talks in the night. We would talk sometimes till morning, till the monks got up to pray. It was the better for that, and for both of us, that we had each other. It can be mighty lonely a lone drunkard in a monastery.

The Captain, still rugged, big-shouldered, his dream to buy a boat, a sailing yacht, and alone with just the sea and the sky to take a trip round the world: 'But I'll never do it.'

He was there, in the monastery for four months before the month I entered and he was four months gone before I followed.

Still we kept in touch and he is a pal. Sober. And writing his story, the longest work and, with that, will say no more about the Captain.

He went, left me in the monastery. Encouraged again by

the literary monk I began to write, pick up on my novel, the tale of a boy-bandit so that as I got over the block, if not easy it was not too hard and I completed the book which turned out to be a different work from what I had intended. But I liked the thing and with some surprise, for the roughest language, the monk did too.

'It's honest,' he said. 'There can be nothing bad in an honest work.'

It took me six hours a day of daily labour, during my remaining four months in the monastery. I had a start during the two months at home, and I mention this six months of work, on a book I loved, to illustrate my sickness.

It would be useless, other than that, apart from that novel for me to dwell on my seclusion, my time in the monastery— I did not drink, I had regrets, but in the book fond hopes for a future.

I returned home to my mother's house, and heard not a word about my drinking, my time in the monastery, Heidi or the kids. After some correction, changes here and there, tender work, I sent the typescript (recorded, I had just one copy) to a London agent.

First days out of the monastery, walking the streets, and it was winter again, grey days, not only the weather, thinking that everyone was looking at me.

Fuck them, I still had spirit. I feared no man, but pity, which I saw in some faces, I could not take.

I would, avoiding pubs and old pals, take long walks and during one of my walks I found a dog. It was a big and ferocious beast, brutalised, with a tail not docked but chopped, and it followed me. I stopped, it stopped, growled a bit but perhaps with some sense that just dogs have, knowing I was as lonely as it, it followed me home.

My heart went out to that dog. It hung back at my door as I teased it in. A monster, monstrosity even, I think a mix of Doberman and Mastiff or Doberman and Rottweiler. It was hard to tell. And I didn't care and I loved that dog, and loved it from the first; I clapped its head, and would have killed the bastard who had chopped, cut off its tail.

It was a good time with that dog on our walks, and I got a job as a watchman, for again wanting to write but needing money, we went to work together.

I wrote a whole new book in the company of that dog. He was a natural guard, big and fierce, but damn near human. To me. We were together all the time, during months when I tried to pull myself together. The only good thing to come out of the ashes, I struggled to write a very weird book. In time when I was trying to sell it, I was given the cold shoulder. A funny book not meant for mirth (though writing it I laughed myself) but a portrait of evil.

I have it yet, that book, *The Rubicon*, written at nights with the dog for company.

I had been in touch with my agent about the other novel. He was impressed. Most. A very fine work. So he said. I was delighted when he sent me the list of authors, and some names I admired, that he had handled. But my book was a tricky one, the subject matter and might take a time for him to place.

I had visions from this letter, of me and the dog in a cottage by the sea. I was sick of the city, my work as a watchman. I saw in my mind's eye, bright mornings, the dog running in front of me, on the hard wet sand near the water's edge.

No booze.

I had wrecked enough, near wrecked myself, in my addiction to the bottle.

Trying to come again, to save some money—and I walked to work and walked home—working seven nights, twelve hour shifts. In a few months I had a few hundred, near to a thousand, and with a bit more sense that money could have gone to a cottage by the sea.

The first drink.

I would not say that I was happy sober, but I would not say of my life till then, that I was ever happy.

Stress.

There was in the book, the novel I had written in the monastery, some stress, the hope that it was published.

I had worked so hard on that book that had there been no stress, there would have been something amiss.

I was optimistic.

Very.

Next time.

But so fucking long.

It took publishers, each one it seemed, about a month at least to reject my book.

And two books now. I had mixed feelings about the latter as though it were either an immense success or total miss. I wrote to the agent, sent him the work, which almost by return he refused to handle. I had not of that book the same love for the first, but thought to see good things in it. I wrote to the agent about the idea of a re-write. He wrote me back that I should forget it, that he was so puzzled by the work, contrast to the last, he had asked for a third opinion. I wrote explaining that the book was seven months of work, nightly labour, and suggested that he should ask for a fourth. By this time my first novel was with Deutsch, and had a fair chance there, so I wrote to my agent asking for their reader's report. Good. The reader wanted the book to be published. I suggested to my agent that he try *The Rubicon* with them, but he, so he said, could not do that, suffer to hawk a book that was shit. In finer language that was the drift of his letter.

I was by then about one year sober and utterly chaste.

It was the longest, by far the longest, I had had no woman, but what time working nights, seven nights and twelve hours a night, had I to get a woman?

Strain.

When I completed the second novel, and I was a father again, another son in Germany, I felt a time-bomb about to explode.

The explosion came when, early one morning—I was coming home from work—my dog was run over and killed.

I cradled its head and it licked my hand and they had to pull me off the driver or I would have killed that man who had killed my dog.

He went to hospital but my dog, the only thing I cared about, which had been truly mine, went in the ground.

It was the end of my sobriety. I was drunk by noon that day and was not at work that night. I could not, no dog, or not just any dog, have faced the night. It was much as Silverfir Street, the tenement tumbling down, the end of an era. To me. I who was no animal lover, I had hated the cat, and had never thought to love a dog.

So I drank. I got drunk, smashed for a week, and the wreckage was impressive.

I phoned my agent with a demand, the bluntest one, for my two books back, and, in rage, a bad mistake, fed the good one to the fire.

Dear fuck, a book would have been published, a work with such care in its pages, toil in each sentence—I remember (and the agent then had it bound, *looking* like a book) the blaze, the heat on my hands and quiet despair as I saw it burn.

Also I had lost my job, told my boss (he owned the factory) to take a fuck—he had come to my door with condolences (another dog lover?) and when would I be back?

'I won't.'

'I know how you feel.'

'I don't think so.' This was the day I had burned my book, and one word led to another and I beat him up and threw him out.

Now this guy was somewhat shady with some gangster pals, and he promised me a thrashing—his word, a thrashing. I laughed. Waited. I did not give a fuck.

I think, with the drink even then, after the first week's drinking, past experience, I knew what I was in for.

However, my thrashing, the two guys he sent, paid money to, I knew. Had known for years, and a thing like this, the man I was, if they harmed me I would go after them—with the booze at this stage, this state of my life, I was good for murder. I just did not care about my life, so worthless anyway, in my eyes so worthless, the struggle I'd had, I was and drinking again, and I didn't much care about another man's life either.

This, feeling that way, is near the bottom of the barrel. They saw and after a couple of drinks decided that it was not worth the money.

A couple of days afterwards I left the city, Glasgow, where even with my mother I felt so fucking Godforsaken.

Suddenly.

The dog gone, taken from me.

The next few months, the recounted tale is a bore of wandering, struggling with the bottle, trying to limit my drinking, to space out the booze so that I did not drink till noon, till I had eaten, and all in all, this crazy run of nippling at it, it would have been better and easier if I had no drink at all.

A couple of drinks just made me mean and wanting more, and as time went on, after some months, I think about nine months of so-called social drinking, I got as drunk as I had ever been. A prolonged binge. Night and morning and through the night. I had no hangovers, I was never sober enough to have hangovers and little sickness. The sickness was that I could drink so much. Whisky and wine. I mixed the two, drank cider or beer or stout. It was all the same.

Brandy or gin or vodka, sherry, I had tried the lot of them in my attempt at social drinking and all of them left me wanting more.

This bout, and bad as it was, I was saved from catastrophe, possibly hospitalisation or a return to the monastery, by a shortage of money.

And back in Glasgow, again with my mother, I thought I'd try AA again.

It was not easy returning to AA. With my pride it was not easy. But, the beauty of that place is they do not turn their back on you. A hundred times a loser they do not turn their back on you.

I got sober for almost a year with the help of AA. I went to meetings four times a week. The first drink. One day at a time. I did not bother with steps or traditions, the first drink, one day at a time, was my commandment. And it might well be that with no time for the rest, the text, I was the loser. I liked the people.

In truth I had quite an interest in the people, or the common problem, if in all honesty I do not think they all had the problem. I would say only one in ten, no more, of that fellowship, had a drinking habit near to alcoholism.

Still, for membership, you need not half-kill yourself like I did.

They say that Alcoholics Anonymous is sobriety without strain. It was anything but for me, but some guys I have spoken to whom I respect, they say it was my own fault, that I had not accepted what I was.

But if I kidded I did it well and was a regular attender for almost a year. Sober, no booze, a supposedly sick man. After my times in the monastery, my long history of booze, I was registered an invalid. Disillusioned. Unhappy. Cynical.

I stopped attending AA. Suddenly. I did not feel at home in the place. Suddenly. As if when it came to my turn to speak I could not think of what to say—you are required to say nothing but expected to say something.

Not fitting in a place where, drinking I had fitted in. Following such a screw-up I began after some weeks away, meetings missed, to drink again. I drank without the slightest remorse, no attempt to fight my weakness. I began morning. Early. A Thursday. Before the pubs were open. I bought a bottle, a litre of wine, and drank it in huge swallows, direct from the bottle.

This a year off drink.

I could make the excuse that I missed, and I did miss the kids in Germany, a son I had never seen and wanted to see. I wanted to see all three of them. But having money enough to go, to visit Germany, I chose to drink.

The litre of wine, my thirst was stirred. As a giant awakening. As soon days went to weeks and weeks to months, I was aware. Drinking fortified wine, gallons of it, near the cheapest plonk but—and with memories of Fingal—it was what I liked and preferred to whisky.

It progressed, that bout, I was gripped by a restlessness near to panic.

Yet I was scared of nothing.

I would wander the streets round strange pubs, drift aimlessly, take trains to Edinburgh and Stirling, Dundee, a lot of places, and a lot of women, who in the morning, in strange beds, I did not know, could not remember meeting.

I ended one night, I remember, though I don't know how, in a darkened room, some eight of us at a spiritualist meeting.

But I ended up in a lot of strange places, strange company, on my jaunts through Scotland, before I went to England.

Birmingham. Where I did slow down. For again, luckily, I was short of money. It would be true of this period that money—the lack of it—was my salvation. I had to work. And working in labouring jobs, for I still was strong, bitter and beat, spiritually lost, but physically strong, I could not drink the way I wished.

Birmingham.

Coventry.

Bristol.

Plymouth.

Many cities, places, seeking but never finding, for what I sought I never found.

I would work for a week or a month, at most in any city for a month, and move on. I'll spare the detail of the models I stayed in, and it was always models, with the shakes I endured, a life of general discomfort, mixing with bums and vagrants of every sort.

But a fast two years.

I was, I am, surprised at the swiftness those years.

But still, I returned, if not to sanity, to Glasgow. I had yet to sample meths.

I was badly down at the heel when I returned to Glasgow in autumn 1978. A return I think which spared me the winter. I had no love for Glasgow. But I had no love for any city or place—I had no love for me. It was then, my life, just constantly drinking, getting drunk when I could, and two years passed as two days, weeks as hours, months as days. My return was a calendar shift, two years older, like a zombie's walk, if a zombie that shook and threw up, my stagger through England. An attempt, a try to lose myself, but it is not, the drinking game, like in the songs—guys beat in love, happy wanderers, train whistles blowing. No. Rather a lost tribe, nothing romantic—there is no romance in sleeping in a model, squalor and filth, till at night, farts and fights in the foulest air, you grow so accustomed that you no longer notice. A dead world. Even if you work, as I worked, as Fingal had worked, as in models many men do work, it is a dead world. Escape exists only in the bottle, which, each sip of it, takes you down that little lower and closer to and the dread of that world, a meths-drinking tramp. There is little escape, way back, you descend, and it is but a step, like a slip in the snow, that fall.

I know guys who have come back, but they are few, and

of the world of the meths-drinker I have no knowledge, though I did drink meths, that vile blue spirit.

But two years passed as weeks, if not days, and I returned home to my mother's house. I again had a beard, but white in the hairs, a peppery bush, I was older if no wiser. No money. Nothing. No watch, clothes, not even a razor—the reason for my beard, and it goes without saying, a thumb-trip home, I had no luggage.

I had to borrow from my mother the price of a bottle and a razor.

Sixteen years old I had returned with gifts, money for her, but at thirty-four I was a beggar.

Autumn, 1978.

My sister lent me money.

I bought more wine.

Lanliq.

El Dorado.

I walked in shoes with holes, no winter coat, *any* coat, to buy the wine.

Lanliq.

El Dorado.

In England I had drunk V.P., Four Crown, but in Scotland, as always, shifted to Lanliq and El Dorado.

And people were talking about me. It is why in Alcoholics Anonymous you are as well to remain anonymous. I was a poor, the worst, advert. How I felt, what feelings I had left, it was as before, that I could take their rage but not their pity. There was something strong, that would not break, and if I would crawl for a bottle it was *all* I would crawl for.

I was again, on my return, on the sick list. It was no problem with my drinking to register sick. And again with barbiturates, tranquillisers, vitamin pills, but what was wrong with me that I needed those things?

I conned the money (spent on wine) to visit a psychiatrist.

There were still some people who sought to help me in Glasgow. And even as I drank the money, my first appointment, this guy shelled out more for another appointment. Wasted money. I clapped eyes on the psychiatrist—he looked like a pink, fat schoolboy—I knew that he could never help me.

It was a grim time and getting grimmer. I could get no work and was sinking.

A morning, winter, snow on the ground, no wine or the money to buy wine, I drank methylated spirit.

A half-pint of it, stuff I had bought, that I could remember buying in better days to clean my typewriter.

I drank just half a pint because there was only half a pint. It was mixed with water, the vilest brew. Still it gave me a lift, rid me of my shakes, and was so much cheaper, more potent than wine. But with guilt I drank it. I was near to tears at where booze had led me, drinking, a hand that shook, the degradation of my fall.

This the FIRST couple of glasses, then—who would know? I finished the half-pint and it seemed quite funny to visit the chemist for my carry-out.

I had the price of methylated spirits, a nice surprise, a couple of bottles. You had to sign a book. Name and address. I must have been reeking of the stuff as I signed the book, bottles, a warning, *not* to drink.

I remember little of my meths-drinking jag. I think it went on a week or so, until I was violently ill, unable to hold it down, unable to hold anything down. The doctor was called for, a stomach upset, a room of fumes and meths smells— how it smells, seeps into your pores—and I swear, as Sebastian shook, as his goatee wagged, that that doctor gagged at the smell of the meths.

I got stuff—a bottle for my stomach and more pills, and if the meths-drinking had lasted a week I was in my bed for two weeks after.

Still that time, those days in bed, they got me sober. For the first time in over two years I was able to think with some clarity, free from alcohol, so something good came of the shameful business.

I would need, not want but need to stop drinking.

Days in bed. Ashamed. In pyjamas bought for me. Long days. I would get up at nights to watch some television, boredom. Drink some tea, eat a bit of toast. I was sick then as ever I had been, as long ago Edward in the old Gorbals had been, and the same woman as nurse, if now her son in place of brother.

I rallied round, tea and toast to soup and chicken. My gut was concave. I took a piss—it smelled of meths, stunk out the lavatory. But I was sober. I remember the first week, anniversary of my last drink of meths, that I was sober. It lent me hope. And as I began to eat I began to get better. Heavier. I had lost in that bout a lot of weight. I began to go out and I had the sensation that I might fall. It was like Dublin all over again, that I had damaged my ear and the same tingle in my fingertips. And older now it took me longer to recover. At least a month before I could walk with no thought to fall, to collapse. Just short walks, visits to the library, this after not just the one week on meths, but accumulated booze, two years of it, of rubbish food, and it took till after Christmas, New Year, that I was fully fit and able to work and to walk long distances.

My visits to the library, the books I read, had me thinking of writing again. This was about three months after the meths-drinking, when with some self-respect I had a job. The most menial one but a job: a book-duster in the library. The head library, Mitchell Street in Glasgow. It paid lousy, the work, and so unusual a task that I might explain. I hoovered the tops of books, long shelves of them, books, judging by the dust in the place, which had not been moved for a hundred years.

This dust stuck in my throat and, a few times, working in the library, I went out for a drink, but just a couple or three pints at most.

The meths drinking, I had no wish to return to that, and

I wanted to write.

Again, and after two years, I wanted to write, and at night I began on a boxing novel that in early summer on the strength of the start, the first few chapters, I won a prize for literature. Fifteen hundred pounds. I had hoped for more, a stay in Portugal, but—feeling jaded, in need of a rest, I went on holiday to Yugoslavia. Dubrovnik. It was the start (that on some Russian vodka, I who did not want to drink, got drunk) of a monster bout.

I was fit if jaded after my try at writing, days in the library, and I went to Yugoslavia. Alone. A bit of peace, some sunshine. So I thought. And I booked one day and went the next. A Sunday night. I was sober, no booze. I had a cup of coffee at the airport. With a pal, the guy who had paid the psychiatrist. But the departure lounge, duty-free, as Aladdin's cave the booze in there. I bought a stock of whisky and wine, whatever they would let me buy. I thought, as in the library, of the pints I had sneaked, that returning no one would know. The booze, whisky I bought was so different from the meths, smooth, hot my chest, a glow in my gut, and drinking from the bottle-neck, a feeling of well-being.

Yugoslavia, Dubrovnik. There was sunshine all right, the bluest sea, nudist islands, women for free, and no shortage of Russian vodka.

A boat took you to a nudist island, and after a morning's drinking, I would sit on a rock and drink the vodka.

It was quite a kick, and there were some beautiful dames, and the sun and the sea and a drop, from that island, in one part, edge, of a good fifty feet to rocks below.

I had bought a pair of sandals that were all that I wore as I slipped and fell and gashed my arm and suddenly dangling, a finger-grip from certain death.

There was no panic, fear, I dangled from the rock, as if

not wanting to die I was not crazy about living.

I swung with no hope to climb up, and the blood from my arm streaked my belly and dripped onto my cock. I felt it drip onto my cock, as I felt the wind and the sun and the strength dreen from my fingers.

Thoughts?

I laughed.

It struck me as awful funny, this life I had led, my death on a nudist island.

But I was rescued by two lesbians, one with thick thighs, a muscled arm and all the power of a man, a strong man, who pulled me up and over.

The lesbians, a helpful pair, found my clothes, and, staggering between them, I was put on the boat to Dubrovnik and, from there, a taxi to the hospital where I got sixteen stitches in my arm.

It is the biggest memory, naked, dangling, a fifty foot drop, a finger hold, a cliff, the sun on my back, blood streaking my belly, dripping onto my cock, my stay in Yugoslavia.

And the lesbians, good women both who saved my life—I toast them now with a sip of coffee.

I got home and I was still drinking. Wine. I drank all of that summer. Wine. I did not write. I could not write. And I lost the book, not a bad start, but I lost it. Almost as though many months later when I tried to pick up on it, it was as the work of a stranger, a man I did not know.

My writing it seemed swung as my moods, my drinking.

The summer went in a blur of wine, but standing up to this punishment, erratic, moody, but bodily strong, no gibbering fool, not outwardly, though my head and my thoughts were a mess. I set off on a trip to Germany.

London.

Paris.

I was drunk in both.

Germany, Koblenz.

It made three.

Cities.

I was drunk in a whole lot of other places, but three cities. With no invite and drinking still I arrived at the town which faced out on the Rhine.

Heidi would not let me in to see the kids. I stayed in an inn, where accidentally, for I had no intention to work, I got a job.

I worked as a street sweeper.

In Germany, the town on the Rhine where I stayed in the inn, drank at nights strong German beer, and limbered up for a legal tussle.

Now there is no civilised country where children, healthy and happy with a loving mother will be taken from her. But a father, and even me, how I was, he has certain rights. And I had a lot to sympathise with, working in Germany, the *natural* father, and it must have been an evil time for Heidi, with me there. Brushing the streets, as though fixed to stay in Germany.

Heidi and I did not speak, though I saw her sometimes, saw the kids, the girl would sneak me looks.

Christ and how I wanted to hold her and her brothers and, with the help of the German court, when I got some custody, I thought of snatching them.

But it was not to be.

A day at my work, I shovelled snow, an overnight fall, the two older children, girl and boy, approached me.

Big-eyed. Blue. The first, close-up, I had seen them. I squatted down.

The girl had long flaxen hair (I am dark) and she looked, from old photos as my mother had looked, and was looking at me with her child eyes. Innocent. Mute. Hand in hand

with her brother, who was smaller, a sturdy little guy, edging
closer to his sister. It almost broke my heart them standing
there, as long ago I had stood hand in hand with my sister,
like him so shy. The memories of good times, innocence, my
sister and me, these my children in a street in Germany,
conjured up.

The snow: the streets, the spires and steeples, cobble-
stones, were all thick with it, white German quilt. Falling.
But a freezing, a hard-cold day for all the snow, blue sky,
and in my work with a shovel I wore gloves, an anorak,
high-laced boots, and I was dressed as a soldier with a
peaked cap, I felt too big and rough and scared to touch
them.

My children.

Heidi hung back, across the way, and I guess she could
not deny me this, nor indeed deny the children, who must
have heard.

They snug, their heads, caps of wool, woollen scarves, the
girl in long woollen stockings, and I thought that they would
never talk.

The boy, I remembered the boy as a baby when he was
just months old and I lulled him asleep with the beat of my
heart. Beating then.

I translated the girl with her big blue eyes saying, 'Are you
our Daddy?'

I wanted to hold and to hug them, I told them yes, I was
their daddy.

The boy, his face aflame, embarrassed and shy, still so
very young, nudged closer to his sister who was not much
older, but so much surer, with eyes that spoke, beautiful
eyes—my mother's eyes, yet my mother's eyes were brown,
not like my daughter's eyes, blue as the sky. It struck me as
strange, same eyes wrong colour.

'We were told you were our daddy.'

I took off the gloves and touched her face with my
fingertips, the ridge of her brow, line of her nose, lips and

chin, a hint of Heidi. Germanic in her mouth and chin, the colour of her hair. She had an easy way and was more confident than I was.

'You want to take us away?'

The boy almost hid behind her now, this strange man, snow-shoveller, come to take them away.

I shook my head. No. I loved them but their place was here, with their mother and baby brother, and it was the first time that I had thought of them as people with a right to live, be happy, and what had I to offer? I loved them but could offer nothing, not then, or offer them only heartache.

Regrets. I am full of regrets. They haunt me sometimes.

I look back on what booze did to me, it took those children from me, and it is the saddest thing—the woe of my life.

I hugged my daughter and my son, so like me at his age, embarassed and shy, and it is the last time, children who did not hug me back, that I have seen them.

But it was about the only noble thing I did in my life, that I walked away, left Germany and all that I loved.

Back in Scotland I still had my job with the library. And I made another attempt to quit on booze. I returned to Alcoholics Anonymous. They had something. There were guys still there and still sober since my first attempt, in the hall in Cunningham Street, the one-eyed guy. I listened most to the members who were a long time sober, the few I thought were alcoholics.

It worked for a while, for some months. And I had bought a bike, an expensive one, with the idea of some exercise, to get myself in shape. There was little exercise at the library. I dusted few books. And I began to cycle to far away AA meetings.

But again I had some notion to write, and with no time with my work in the library and the AA meetings, one had to go. I quit the AA meetings. A bad mistake, I should have quit the library, a job of stale days which was getting me down.

I was sober then, spring, for a few months, and was able to manage my life, sleeping soundly and eating like a horse.

Physically, booze had harmed me little, if at all.

But I stopped going to the AA meetings, continued to work, or posed as working, dusting books, while at nights I wrote, tried hard to pick up on the boxing book.

But the bastard would not go, I just could not move it, and when in desperation I did, the writing was no good. I knew it was no good, but I continued to the end. Bitter. Both the end and me and with the loss of the novel I began to drink again.

I bought two litres of wine and the same of cider and drank them in the morning. By this time the book was done and I had finished with the library, a job which near drove me to drink, and if little money I had plenty of time.

In the midst of this I went again to Yugoslavia, for another tangle with the Russian vodka. But a supposed two-week holiday, lasted only a week. I was attacked by a swarm of mosquitoes that almost killed me.

I returned to Glasgow stung from head to toe, my system poisoned, and ended up in the casualty ward of the Victoria Infirmary. With my sister. We were close, my sister and I, we always were, still are. She who never drank. So alcoholism, my mother and sister, my father, it would not seem hereditary.

In the event, the bites, the booze, Russian vodka, the doctors—there were three of them—wanted verification and observation of my complaint, so that, in a bed in a ward, I remained two days.

I would not hear of it, two days without a drink. They gave me an injection, a note to take to my own doctor, and the warning not to drink.

Impossible.

For sick as I was, I had not forgotten to smuggle some booze, five bottles or six of the Russian vodka.

So a night's drinking to awake next day a monster. Truly. One eye closed, the other closing, my head a torture of lumps and bumps.

It did not stop me drinking; I had all the more reason to drink, to try to forget the thing. But that was difficult and time went on, after some hours the remaining eye closed and I drank blind, a feel for the bottle.

I had to call the doctor in.

I was drunk as a skunk when he came, but that was no surprise, that man, who at this point was well used to me and my drinking.

He gave me a prescription for some pills, and again the warning not to drink, though again I did drink. But not for long. No. Whatever my ailment, those pills when I drank I was spewing sick and it might well be that the doctor who knew me knew that.

So again I was on the wagon. A hellish week. I hurt, a mass of bites from my toes to the top of my head. One night when I was all but driven crazy with itch, I poured a bottle of Lysol over my head. If the thing had gone on, such misery, I would have poured a bottle of Lysol down my throat. And it was so hard, difficult, the splash of a bath, the hope to kill the itch, that I soon wished I had stayed in hospital where there was some assistance with a bath.

I had by now no urge to drink and by the time I recovered had lost the desire to drink.

I went back, though I don't know why, or perhaps for there was nothing better, for where else could I go, to Alcoholics Anonymous.

This time I did fit in and got to like the meetings, take an interest in the people, though I still could not talk, express myself and how I felt. If I felt blue I would kid myself I was happy.

That programme, I worked it all wrong, I did not work

it at all, and yet for spells it helped keep me sober, away from that first and fatal drink.

This time, given my sickness and mosquito bites, I quit drinking in better shape than before. There was no hangover. I had been too sick, a general discomfort, for the usual symptoms, and the bout cut short, nothing sustained—it required time from the fiercest drinking. I suffered badly from the shakes, sweats and hallucinations. So my illness, mosquitos or what, I got off drinking easy that time.

But again when I tried to write I could not write, string three words to four. I could write a letter, but creative writing, the work of a story, it was no good. Nothing. What I wanted to do. Though why, the art, the toughest one, with lonely effort and small reward, I wanted to be a writer is a mystery.

It is still a mystery.

The hardest work.

Writing, and even in the monastery when I was writing well, prolifically, it was easily the hardest work I had ever done.

But it would not go, there was some block, choked head, and I gave up on it and wrote nothing, not a word all of that summer. Sober. It was worse sober unable to write. With booze I had an excuse. Still on bike rides, long ones, I soon thought nothing of a hundred miles; I grew fit and sharp. Supple. I became a master cyclist. Hardly surprising as I was always with my bike. It was something like a faithful dog, but I drank again and I smashed it—I smashed and wrecked that bike as by my drinking I had smashed and wrecked lives with a total disregard.

I do not know, I did not count the period of my abstinence. Ten weeks or twelve, something like that, but enough I remember to give mother some hope. Her mad son. Who, and again I had money from a big win on the first Leonard–

Duran fight, hit the bottle for no reason at all, or merely boredom.

It might have been boredom.

I had no job and could cycle only so much, and though I advertised for a lady companion (I got two replies to my advert for a riding companion, but won't go into that) I cycled alone, no company.

Days sometimes under a hot sun, a run down the coast, I would feel like a beer. Nothing desperate, no craving, but a notion for some beers, and the first was a drink in Troon. On the Ayrshire coast. Where once as a boy in short pants I had spent a holiday of some days. And some nostalgia in the town, the beach, the boy who was me, I hoisted a few.

I did not get drunk, I cycled home. With a couple more beers, stops on the way, I cycled home.

But it was the start, and the next day I was drinking more and drinking whisky. I got drunk next day. And the next. And then drinking wine, litre bottles.

This was September, late August—I am not sure, but I drank all through September to November, when in the bicycle crash, I broke my right hand. I crashed the bike on a Thursday night but it was the Sunday before I thought to go to hospital, have it fixed, a double fracture. I was so drunk. And continued, my hand in a plaster cast, to drink some more. Cold nights then, approaching winter, and I had a big bet, almost all that I had on Roberto Duran to beat Sugar Ray Leonard in their return fight. I was never so sure of the result of a fight, which was no fight, and I was so enraged by Duran's surrender, the money I'd lost, that I crashed my good hand through the kitchen window.

My right hand still in the plaster cast, a bottle of wine, drinking all night and all morning, just my mother and me, I tore the left hand badly. Ripped an artery. Blood spurted to splash the roof and paint the walls. My face was full of it. So suddenly in a moment of rage at the beaten Duran. I swathed the hand in two towels, best as I could, but again, and not a week between this and the broken hand, I made a visit to the hospital.

Sitting there in the casualty ward, my mother and me, the blood seeping the towels and dripping on the ground, I ranted against Duran.

I could have lost the hand yet I ranted against Duran. They wrapped the wounds with a mighty bandage. White. I forget how many stitches, but the bandage was white. All the weight and bulk of a boxer's glove.

So both hands now.

It was an effort to open the taxi door on the way home. A taxi I stopped to buy more wine. About eight bottles. Litres. The assistant had to carry them out. I got home and the driver had to carry them in. I think, I must have known by the state I was in, that it was next to impossible to go out myself and buy more wine.

But with the blood I had lost, and I had lost a lot of blood, I was too tired to drink and went to bed on my return from the hospital.

This was about noon, no later, and I slept till late, near midnight, when I was awoken by the pain in my hand, the grip of the stitches.

It was not easy to get dressed, pull on a pair of trousers.

A shave, even to wash, was out of the question and a shit was a trial. Such a feeling of impotence, vulnerability, trouble of a shit, to brush my teeth. And self, or booze inflicted, no fight or nothing, and it was a subdued drink I drank at midnight.

And yet one of my best drinks. It will be hard I fancy for the tee-totaller or modest imbiber to understand that still stained with blood, sore, the stitches in my hand, it was one of my best drinks. Midnight. Alone. Some fumble to fill the glass. But it was, sitting in the still of the house thinking things over, and I had a lot to think over. How after my losing the bet was I to get out of this fix? I filled the glass time and again with the sticky harsh wine. Thinking.

Money. I was in a financial bind after my bet on Duran, and useless, helpless as a child with two ruined hands.

I should mention, for what it is worth, that so confident was I of my bet on Duran, that I had a case half-packed, the thought of a holiday, a stay in Cyprus.

It should serve too to show the size of my bet. Beaten. As I was beaten by booze, for I knew it then that night, and even drinking, that booze had won, beat me to the floor, that much more of it would chase me to the grave.

Yes, a sobering drink, and that part of its charm that it was a sobering drink for all the bottles, litres of wine.

I smoked and drank and thought what to do, but could do nothing, not with my hands the way I was, a cripple.

Not young, not old, but no way young, the best years and the vent of youth behind me. Gone. Lost forever in a blur of booze. And I hated the stuff then that night, the things I had lost, even as I drank it. Yet still not prepared to give it up—the stuff had given me only despair.

I drank the wine. In the dark. Just the glow of the street-lights, and thought of writing that I wanted to do, a couple of novels, some thought of the book I had burned and the idea to write it again.

But firstly I required money. Money fast.

I will not even hint at how I got the money.

Suffice to say, that I had retained my wits and was wily enough. Booze had stolen a lot, almost taken my life, but I could still think.

I could think of my children in Germany and how I missed and wanted them. Indeed that night in my silent drink I ached to hold them. I drank the best of a litre of wine and after a couple of pills went back to bed. A drugged sleep. Deep.

I awoke feeling better than I had any right to feel.

But again dressing, one hand in a cast, a mighty bandage on the other, was a fucker.

There was comfort though that my wounds would heal,

that in two weeks or three I would have full ten fingers again.

And money.

Not a fortnight after the defeat of Duran I had more money than before, almost as much as if he'd won. And when I got the use of my hands I began to drink in pubs, whisky and beer, all-day sessions, and I thought of Germany and my children. I thought of them all the time. Night after night in the mornings. Girl and boy and baby boy so far from me, my loving arms. And I cursed Heidi, her father, the whole stinking crew in Germany, the town on the Rhine.

This period, a time of gloom, was too a time of the heaviest drinking.

No fun, punishment, shakes and sweats, but the mess of my life and my children lost. I who could feel, who stumbled as lost, who in Germany was taken for an animal. I could not live without the bottle, comfort, drunk, that made you forget it all, the people you loathed, who loathed you, the sweats and shakes, a morning poke that had you wish to die.

I was terribly disturbed by this drinking, nightmares and the like, and on a particularly bad morning after a particularly bad night I went round to see the priest.

This was a pious man, nothing phoney, and there are phoney priests, men with no right to wear the cloth, and if I did not share his views, believe in God, I did respect the man.

It was a dreadful time, it had to be a dreadful time to have me visit a priest. Who was understanding, knowing, a worldly head if a closeted life, and I would visit him drunk finding some sedation in his presence.

I managed again with the help of this priest, a quiet way with his help, an almighty struggle, to stop drinking.

Two weeks I lasted.

I was hardly rid of the shakes, back to proper eating when I started all over again.

A couple of whiskies that went to a few, two more litres

of the harsh cheap wine that very night.

Dear Christ above, don't you know I'm pining—and tears did fall from my eyes.

Mornings.

Grim light. Winter. It was now December. I would sit at home most of the day drinking wine. It was seldom that I bothered with pubs, just perhaps buying the wine I might sink some beers. But I had not in this drinking my former drouth, that urge for beer. A couple of cans might do me all day. It was a fucked-up life, fucked-up by drinking, all upside down, like that the wine was beer and the beer was wine.

1980, near 1981.

Had anyone told me in 1960—in the model in Manchester, the winter that year I had come home ...

Yet I looked at myself. I brushed my teeth, I still had all my hair and nothing bloated, it seemed only my head that the stuff was rotting. But rotting it bad, the thoughts I had. In a smouldering rage I drank the wine and thought about Germany.

I would sometimes nights after long days in the house go out a stroll, and saw the first Christmas trees and I had a thought this season, goodwill, to play it to the hilt.

I bought some toys, a trip to Germany.

It saddens me still, the toys I bought, the man I was, my thought, the weirdest Santa Claus, the joy the kids—if only the toys, not me, my appearance would cause on Christmas morning.

I was in fine humour as I went round the stores and bought the toys. I chose with care. And a fine collection, money no object, a full bag of them, things I thought kids would like, I waited for Christmas.

Drinking. Laughing. I phoned the Samaritans. The lady at the other end, she thought it a fine idea, and it was good to talk to an anonymous voice, a lady who thought it a fine idea.

The month wore on. I was impatient.

First I thought to fly but I was so impatient and eager I changed my route to overland. Like that in the very act of moving, going, I might bring Christmas sooner, be there a little quicker.

Night train. How many now night trains, London to Glasgow and back again? I stumbled aboard with a grip and my bag of toys.

Needless to say I had wine in my grip and a hangover when I awoke in London.

Euston Station.

It was changed now, since I had first come, visits since, an off-sales in the station, no need for the grocer's in Euston Road.

But walking the platform of this station, if I had been sad before, that morning I had a new experience of the meaning of sadness. It engulfed me like a giant's arms. My pitiful toys. I was still too numbed, too recent my drinking, last night, to sweat or shake, but with a cracking head I sat in the station.

It was warm, the station, that long ago had a wind from the rails, the streets outside and I remembered as freezing, as granite and stone, not as now all plastic and rubber, cosy as an airport lounge.

I sat and smoked and it was useless. There might, was I lucky, be other days, times, but now was not that day or time. It was the first time in many days sitting in that Station that I found a bit of self-respect. At what cost some self-respect? Four hundred miles from home, the Samaritan who with a surprisingly young and chirpy voice, had after days of wine urged me on to a plot I knew at the root of me would never work. Yet I had hoped so desperately, willed self-deceit that it might work.

'They are your children,' the Samaritan had said, 'you have every right to visit them.'

But what did she know of life, the man she was speaking

to, a cunning man just using her, almost knowing the words that she would say, but knowing too, as I must have known by the very act of phoning her that buying the toys, my happiness was illusionary, a thing, how things stood, that just could not be. But sad to fool myself to happiness. That rebounded now, inside of Euston Station.

There was something unreal in the morning, yet more vivid than any, the milling crowds, rush hour, people going to work, I sat with my bag of toys drinking slugs of wine.

I must have slept for, too soon it was near to midday and the station was empty and bigger.

There was a couple of cops looking at me, but I was not badly clad, good shoes and coat, I looked at them and they looked away.

I felt no shame, the cops, my wine, rather fuck it, that I could sit where I wanted and drink if I wished.

But I was more sober now and the pitiful toys, a sense of self-loathing at the sham, excuse for a man I had become. I could not rid myself of my self-deceit, self-loathing after my talk with the Samaritan. I was ashamed of that, my talk with the Samaritan, no man at all, the man I should be, had me here, stuck as though glued to a seat in Euston Station.

I drank more wine, a giant swallow, about a half-pint swallow so that I almost threw up. I had to hold my breath to keep it down. First swallow. You felt it in the pit of your gut, cold and hard, solid, like a brick down there, before as dissolving, you felt the heat spread out.

A couple more swallows, I went for a piss. I left the toys but took the grip, some bottles of wine, I went for a piss.

In Euston Station.

There are a lot of fly guys in Euston Station, a lot of fly guys in any station, but when I returned, the toys which I had hoped had gone, vanished, still sat. Forlorn. They looked as forlorn as I felt, walking in a station I hated towards them.

I had about nine hundred pounds. Cash. In my wallet.

And that was all that I had, for no bank account, no nothing, just a bag of toys, the clothes that I wore, and a bunch of creditors.

The toys, and a train-set alone, had set me back two hundred pounds. At least two hundred pounds, to have then if ever lost children I loved, the truth crashed down about me.

I sat, drank the wine, as so often in so many places I had sat and drank, whisky or wine, a whole stack of brews, sherry to rum to meths.

And where the fuck had they taken me? Almost Christmas, almost (though it seemed impossible) thirty-seven, sitting alone in Euston Station.

I drank all through the day and into the night, the workers, morning commuters returning, me still sitting. Drinking. Hardly drunk but far from sober. An even edge. And the day flew. Past. Night. Some flurry in the station, the workers returning, returning home.

But where dear fuck was home for me? I who, in my life of wasted days had had so many homes, pillows to lay my sodden head.

I watched the people, gents, long winter coats, their bowler hats, umbrellas, careers, wives and children, and for the first time, such people, mundane lives, I envied them.

Secure?

Content?

Happy?

Any one, a half of one, was much richer than me.

Six o'clock, the station clock—I had no watch.

Seven.

The station was quiet.

A porter—how now many porters?—swept about my feet.

I had sat for more than twelve hours, and all of that time I had sat alone. Smoking. Drinking. I had shifted a couple of litres of the strong harsh wine.

But still not drunk. A sore arse from my long time sitting, but not drunk. My head, my eyes held focus. Thought. Reason.

Eight o'clock.

Some young ones now brushed and scrubbed, lean boys, curvy girls, and still I sat.

Nine o'clock.

I opened a new, last bottle of wine. And drinking this one faster, like a flourish, queer pride, for it was as if all of my days they had led me here, this day, this station, and I wanted to go out in style.

Ten o'clock.

I was drunk by ten o'clock.

With a definite stagger I crossed the station to buy a ticket, a return to Glasgow.

I returned to the seat where the toys still sat. I left them sitting. A zig-zag lurch, the station tilting, I left the toys, my grip, empty bottles, and a bit of the demon, I think, I left in Euston Station, London.